D1525706

COPP ON ICE

COPP ON ICE

Don Pendleton

DONALD I. FINE, INC.
NEW YORK

Manufactured in the United States of America

10 9 8 7 6 5 4 3 2 1

Designed by Irving Perkins Associates

This novel is a work of fiction. Names, characters, places and incidents are either the product of the author's imagination or are used fictitiously. Any resemblance to actual events, locales, organizations or persons, living or dead, is entirely coincidental and beyond the intent of either the author or publisher.

Library of Congress Cataloging-in-Publication Data
Pendleton, Don.
Copp on ice / Don Pendleton.
p. cm.
ISBN 1–55611–235–1
I. Title.
PS3566.E465C67 1991
90–56069
CIP
813'.54—dc20

For Jay and Lillie,
who know how to take charge
and are doing so. Keep on.

"They who are of the opinion that Money will do everything, may very well be suspected to do everything for Money."

—GEORGE SAVILE,
Marquess of Halifax

"I regard sex as the central problem of life."

—HAVELOCK ELLIS,
Psychologist

"If it were not for money and sex, we would not need cops."

—JOE COPP,
American Private Investigator

CHAPTER 1

SHE WAS VERY PRETTY, with long golden hair and a dazzling smile, tall—about five-ten—beautifully tanned and outfitted in a tight denim skirt and silken blouse unbuttoned to an enticingly shiny decolletage—very graceful in her movements. I figured "dancer or athlete" in my instant appraisal. It's my business to appraise people, all kinds of people—not just beautiful women—so it's like a conditioned response for me to get a size on people in that first look. Not that I'm always right, but usually close enough.

I did not have this one sized, however, in the Most Important Perspective. That MIP tries to differentiate between friend and foe, danger and pleasure, truth and fiction. I saw only a very attractive woman—maybe a dancer or athlete—approaching with a dazzling smile as I wrestled a few sacks of groceries into my car outside the supermarket. It seemed that she intended to accost me. I admit that I am readily accostable in such circumstances, especially so in the warm sunlight of a beautiful day at a peaceful shopping center, and of course I had no idea . . .

"Aren't you Joe Copp?" she asked me in an interestingly accosting voice from about two paces out.

I have never tried to deny it. But then I am also no celebrity. I was doing a quick scan of memory and finding nothing familiar there as I closed the car door and turned to meet that greeting. "That's me. Have we met, I hope?"

Her smile instantly lost its dazzle then vanished completely. Out of the corner of an eye I saw a car moving slowly toward me along the traffic lane in a way that definitely registered a negative on my MIP scale while the blonde assaulted it from the front. She ripped her blouse open with a quick jerk that sent suddenly unfettered boobs into a freedom dance, let out a shriek, and flung herself onto me. Hell, I was trying to push her away but it must have looked like just the opposite—and, of course, that was the intention.

This is a very popular shopping center. There were people all around. I'm surprised I didn't get mobbed, then and there. Maybe I would have, because I couldn't get her off and she was raising a hell of a ruckus. I'm thinking, "Jesus . . ." when this car swerves in alongside and two big guys jump out. They're cops, I know they're cops because I've been a cop all my life and I know a cop when I see one, no matter how he's dressed. I'm trying to tell them that the thing is not the way it looks—will they please take this crazy woman off me? But they just put me in an armlock while the blonde is still trying to knee me. Next thing I know, I'm in handcuffs and being stuffed into the back seat of their car while one of the cops is talking to the woman. A crowd has gathered and I am getting curious looks from every quarter.

There is not time for much of that, though, because very

quickly—entirely too quickly—both cops are in the car and we are driving away.

I knew already—or suspected very strongly—that it was a setup. I was being hustled. But why? The guy at the wheel kept giving me glances through the rearview mirror. The other sat sidewise in the front seat and kept me fixed with a hard stare. I didn't intend to play that game. After a couple of blocks, I said, "Police station's the other way, guys."

"Shut up," said Sidewise.

"Get screwed," I said back. "You've no intention of booking me so let's get it settled quick. A gallon of ice cream is melting on my groceries. So give me the message while you're taking me back to my car."

The driver swerved abruptly toward the curb, stopped the car, swiveled about to give me a long, hard stare before telling me, "You'll fucking *walk* back to your car, asshole. This's no taxi service."

"Maybe you'd better tell me what it is, then."

His partner showed me a thin smile, said, "Maybe we'd better take you out to the gravel pit and teach you some humility."

These are both big guys. I'm six-three and way beyond two hundred pounds, but these guys were bigger. Of course, size advantage is mainly in the mind. My Judo master is roughly the height and weight of an average American ten-year-old, he's seventy-five years old, and he'd already taught me a lot of humility.

"I'm humble enough," I told these guys. "Forget the gravel pit. The point is made. I'm vulnerable. Any one of you guys can get my license any time you want it. I understand. So who's mad at me now?"

The guy at the wheel smiled suddenly and told

me, "Nothing personal, Joe. Hey, we respect you. That's the whole point. We respect you enough to tell you in advance, see. There's enough trouble in Brighton already. A celebrity-type P.I. nosing around will just muck things up even worse."

I'd been called many different kinds of private cop but never that one. I said, "Thanks for the casting but we're a long way from Brighton right now and I probably don't see the town twice a year. So thanks. I can safely assure you that I will not be nosing around any time soon."

"That's good, because if we were in Brighton right now you'd be on your way to the dungeon right now. Anything can happen to a guy, any time. Right? Like right out in front of the grocery store. Never know. It sometimes comes from nowhere. Blam! You're in the pokey. Never knew what hit you."

I tried to smile as I replied, "Two big shiny jugs hit me, pal. Give the lady my regards. Where does she work? Maybe I'd like to see more of what she's got."

"Nah, you wouldn't. Lila wears handcuffs on her belt and a sap in her panties."

"So you're telling me where she works. Same place you work."

"Sidewise" produced an ID and held it up for my inspection. Brighton Police Department. "We're just trying to take care of business, Joe. You know the routine. Just don't get caught up in it."

I said, "Yeah . . . you do have problems in Brighton."

So they did. Hardly anyone living in Southern California could have escaped notice of that. Something new in the press almost daily for months. Mayor murdered with a prostitute in a sleazy motel. Chief of Police fired amid rumors of rampant corruption in his department. City Attorney resigned, City Administrator resigned, recall petitions being circulated to remove councilmen, political turmoil in every area of city government—it had been a mess for a long time. It's one of the old foothills cities at the eastern edge of the Los Angeles basin, sleepy little village for most of its life before the population boom sent the big city developers scurrying for virgin lands to convert into housing tracts. Now even these relatively remote areas are bursting at the seams and struggling for stability in the face of continuing pressures for further development. When I first came south a mere ten years ago, Brighton had a population of about thirty thousand. Now it's close to a hundred thousand. And, yeah, hurting.

I told my new pals from Brighton, "I have no clients in your town. So I don't know why you guys drove all the way over here to tell me your troubles. Not that I don't sympathize. I simply have no interest there. So . . . my ice cream."

"Can't do that yet," Sidewise told me.

"When can you?"

"When you tell us who your client is."

I tried to spread my hands in a gesture of innocence, and was reminded that they were still cuffed behind me. "I'm working two cases right now," I confided. "One is for a public defender in Pomona who thinks his client is innocent on a drugs-related murder charge and hopes I can produce evidence that he is. He's guilty as sin but you guys would have no interest. The other case is an insurance scam, nothing to do with the problems in Brighton. Now can we rescue my groceries?"

"Why are you lying to us, Joe?" asked the guy at the wheel, in a friendly tone. "We know you've been retained. Our information is solid. So why are you treating us this way?"

"Maybe it's these cuffs," I replied in the same friendly

5

tone. "I don't think well with my hands behind my back."

"Oh, shit!" Sidewise exclaimed. "Forgot all about that!" He slid outside, opened my door and pulled me out, spun me around and pushed my head onto the roof, took off the cuffs, hit me in the small of the back with a knee and took me in a choke-hold, spun me out onto the sidewalk and kicked me in the side as I was going down.

He was back inside the car and it was moving away before I raised my head off the cement.

I wasn't mad. I was thankful that it came out so easy. Had a couple of sore spots and a somewhat shaken sense of dignity, but all in all . . . not so bad, not so mad.

The mad would come later, after I'd had awhile to think about it.

I hoofed it on back to the supermarket, got in my car, and got the hell away from there. I live only five minutes away, in the hills overlooking the urban sprawl known as the San Gabriel and Pomona valleys, east of Los Angeles. Brighton is about twenty minutes farther east, toward San Bernardino. I'd really had no interest in that town, never had, never expected I would.

But now I did.

Those guys could not have done a better job if they'd been trying to lure me there. I may have told you that I've been a cop all my adult life. A public cop for more than fifteen years, with some damned big departments—San Francisco, Los Angeles, and Los Angeles County Sheriff's Departments. Worked it all, did it all—traffic, burglary, vice, narcotics, homicide, SWAT—learned it all but never really got comfortable with the politics that go with it, finally decided to do my own thing my own way, went private, pick my own jobs now and make my own way. It's not always fun, not always challenging, and it's never secure. But it's my life and I'm in charge of it, and I like it that way.

Never expected to be in charge of a department. The mere suggestion of any such possibility would be a laugher, for sure.

I had told those Brighton cops the truth. I had not been retained to do anything in or concerning their town. But they'd set me up for it, sensitized me to it. So when the new city administrator for Brighton called me at home that night and offered me the job, I took it without thinking twice.

Not a retainer, no. A job. He wanted me to take a temporary appointment as Chief of the Brighton Police Department.

I took it.

And then I laughed. Which shows how dumb I can be sometimes.

CHAPTER 2

CARL GARCIA IS A QUALITY GUY. We'd never been what you'd call friends, exactly—not in the sense of visiting in each other's homes or hitting the town together, hadn't been anything like that. But I guess we'd always liked and respected each other, and a friendship like that can sometimes be more compelling than the other kind.

We met in San Francisco while I was on the force there and he was a civilian police administrator. Within that year I was walking out the door and heading south in a graceful exit to join LAPD with my good record intact, thanks to a courageous stand by the good Garcia when all around him were howling for my scalp. I think that cost him, though he never said anything about it, because he was out the door himself a few months later and working for one of the smaller Bay Area cities in a similar capacity. That usually means smaller pay—so, yeah, it cost him.

We hadn't actually made an effort to keep in touch across the years—wasn't that kind of friendship—but circumstances kept us crossing paths now and then during the course of business. He'd moved around some too. That can happen to a quality guy who won't play the games some would demand of him. Somewhere in those years he'd picked up a master's degree in government administration; last I'd heard of him, I was with L.A. County and he was City Manager for one of the inland Northern California towns. I sent announcements around to everyone I've ever known when I set up my own shop as a cop for hire, so of course I sent one to Garcia, too, but never knew if he'd received it because we'd been out of touch for a couple of years.

You can imagine my surprise, then, when Carl called me that Friday evening from the Brighton city hall and offered me a job. *Temporary* job, he hastened to point out, good for probably no more than seventy-two hours, or until the city council could bury their own differences long enough to get together and shoot down the appointment. And of course they would. Candidates for a job like this are screened very carefully, qualifications weighed and reweighed, salaries negotiated and all that. They'd shoot it down.

But there was big trouble in Brighton, for sure. Carl had been hired by the council just a few days earlier. His predecessor had resigned at the height of a political firestorm which also took the police chief's job, one week after the death of the city's mayor. I'd never known Carl Garcia to be afraid of anything but he sounded nervous and maybe even a bit scared. "I have to emphasize, Joe, that you'll be walking into a pressure cooker that no man in his right mind would want to contend with. And it could be dangerous. The whole thing here is thoroughly rotten. I'm actually afraid of the cops here, and I believe a couple of the councilmen are certifiably insane."

10

"Why hire me," I managed to ask, "when you know I'll be fired almost immediately?"

"Well, I guess you must know that I'll expect you to come over here and kick some asses into line in your usual direct approach to problem-solving. I—"

"You know that I've gone private."

"Yes. I received your announcement. Took awhile because you sent it to the wrong place. By the time it caught up with me it was too late to send congratulations, so what the hell, congratulations I guess if that's the way you want it. I'm not asking you to give anything up. It's just that I can't call a private eye in here to kick ass in the police department—not as a private eye, that is. You've always been a lightning rod, Joe. I figure you'll draw enough lightning over the weekend to at least get a feeling for who can and cannot be trusted in this town. Just give me a handle, even a very short one."

"Who's running the department at the moment?"

"I am," he said ruefully.

"You don't have an acting chief?"

"They're all Indians here, Joe; no chiefs."

I didn't like the sound of that. "I couldn't go along with a sham appointment," I told him.

"Neither could I," Garcia assured me. "It's strictly legal. I get to run the city until the council unleashes veto power. They're so disorganized it will take them awhile to do that. If I want you to run the PD, then by God you'll run it your way until someone yanks both of us out. Will you do it?"

"You want me to kick ass."

"That's what I want, yes."

"Cops too."

"Cops especially."

"You sound worried."

11

"I am worried. There have been death threats, Joe."

"Against you?"

"Against my wife and kids. They're still up north and that makes it even worse. I haven't found a place to live down here yet, still in a hotel."

"Stash them."

"Right now?"

"Soon as you break this connection, yes. Put them into cool storage, right now. Tell no one where they're at, not even Grandma, and use a public phone to send them there. Once they're stashed, don't let them use a credit card or a telephone. They are to get cool and stay that way. Understand? Maybe it's an overreaction, and let's hope it is. But do it."

"Okay, yes, I'll do that. Does this mean you're taking the job?"

"That's what it means, yes. When do I start?"

"I was hoping you could come right now. The timing is important. I figure we need the weekend to sneak you in past the council."

I sighed, checked the clock, and told him, "Give me a couple of hours."

The relief was evident in his voice. "Right. I'll be waiting. Come straight to city hall, Chief."

After I hung up I sat there for a couple minutes, staring at the telephone. *Chief,* eh? It was a laugher. The rest was not. It all sounded a bit nutty and unbelievable, but I'd been hearing things out of Brighton and I knew it was all entirely ominous too. But I laughed anyway, remembering Sidewise, Taxidriver, and Lila Boobs.

It was worth a laugh, sure.

I could cry later . . . and I would.

* * *

Brighton sits low in the foothills with a view of Mt. Baldy and several other towering peaks of the San Gabriel and San Bernardino mountains. In the winter, they're snowcapped peaks and nothing is prettier. Rest of the time they just stand there shrugging off the desert heat and smog rising from below, sometimes shrouding themselves with cooling clouds when conditions are right—and sometimes the Santa Anas whistle down their slopes and scream through the canyons of the foothill communities like angry spirits from some long gone Indian tribe hoping to discourage the steady encroachment of the squatters filling the broad valleys and blotting out the hills, but nothing will discourage that except maybe a couple of well-timed 8.2 quakes arising from the numerous faults that crisscross the area.

The city was founded by agricultural pioneers before the turn of the century. They brought year-around water to the desert and transformed it into garden oases of citrus and avocado, date and olive and grape, built packing sheds and rail lines and roadways, tamed the wilderness and prepared it for the urban onslaught that would follow a hundred years later. Gone now are most of the crops, the packing sheds, the farm laborers camps and most everything else related to agriculture, replaced by broad boulevards usually choked with endless streams of cars and trucks, square mile upon square mile of houses and apartments and restaurants and service stations, liquor stores and theaters, shopping malls to stupefy those early pioneers, and problems no suburban city ever thought it would have to face.

Ten years ago the Brighton Police Department numbered thirty sworn officers and four civilian employees. Police excitement in those days would involve little more than a fistfight in a local bar, a fenderbender on Main street or a rowdy drunk beating up his wife. Today you can count nearly a hundred badges, a civilian bureaucracy almost as large as the sworn force ten years ago, and they deal routinely with gang drive-by shootings, armed robberies and burglaries, a homicide rate that has doubled in two years, drug dealers large and small, rapes and violence of every type, prostitution, sophisticated white-collar crimes and cons and swindles; name it, they got it at Brighton just as in any big city in the land, and all in a dizzying ten years.

What they did not have at Brighton at the time was an effective police department. What they had was a department in shambles, no clear direction, no morale, no faith in their ability to police the town. And of course it goes without saying, in such a situation, they had some b*aaa*d cops on that force. I could smell them all over the place, like stinking garbage that's hidden away and you can't see it but God you know it's around somewhere close.

I hit town about an hour before midnight, traveling light with only a suit bag and a few changes of underwear, and met briefly with Carl Garcia in his office. He swore me in, gave me my badge and gun, walked me over to the PD and introduced me to the watch captain, and then he left town for parts unannounced.

The captain's name was McGuire, they called him Pappy, and he clearly did not like me for shit. Which was okay, I didn't like him either and it meant not a thing either way. He had twenty officers coming in for the graveyard shift and a few more than that going off; I ordered them all to stay put and told McGuire I wanted a general muster of every sworn badge within the hour, no exceptions except for those presently engaged in sensitive duty operations. He gave me a nasty look and I thought for a quick staredown minute there that he was going to disregard the order, but finally he blinked first and passed the command along to the dispatch office.

It was a modern, clean, and spacious building outfitted with all the latest technology. These cops obviously wanted for nothing that money could buy. They had a workout gym and a couple of handball courts, luxurious lounge, all the employee trappings of an enlightened and prosperous city. What had gone so sour?

My office was a marvel. The desk was as big as a double bed. Had a long leather couch, a little alcove with tables and four overstuffed chairs—a television and a VCR, for God's sake—even a full bath with glassed-in shower stall. A snazzy hi-tech communications unit was built flush into the desk; you could audit all the telephones from there and record conversations, patch in directly to the dispatcher's console and record there too. I'd never seen anything like it, certainly had not expected to see it in Brighton, of all places.

I decided I could live there, at least for the weekend, brought my stuff in from the car and set up my shop, then went out for a word or two with Pappy McGuire. He's a guy about forty, long and lean, frown wrinkles rumpling the forehead, all the negative elements of a cop's eyes—suspicion, fear, worry, hostility—you can't miss it and you can't overlook it.

He asked me right off the top, "You been certified by the research and academic council for this job?"

He was referring to a state organization that establishes training criteria and qualifications for police management positions as an aid to local governments. "Not lately," I replied. "You?"

"Two years ago. Why do they always want to go outside the department for a new chief? I'll have to uproot if I want to go any higher in this line of work. Not that it

15

wouldn't be better after all, considering the loonies at *this* city hall."

"They didn't even appoint you Acting Chief," I said, watching for his reaction. "Why not?"

McGuire shrugged, picked at his nose, examined his fingernails. "They appointed nobody Acting Chief. It's been a revolving situation, with each Watch Commander as the badge in charge reporting directly to the City Administrator, except that we had no C.A. until your friend Garcia arrived. It's no job for a civilian, I guess even you know that. We figured Garcia to do something stupid. Looks like he's done it. Where'd you come in from? What's your background?"

"San Francisco," I replied casually. "LAPD, L.A. Sheriff's, cop for hire. What's yours?"

He gave me a startled look. "I've been here my whole career."

"That's steady," I said. "Or dumb. Which is it?"

"More and more I think it's dumb," McGuire told me quietly. He scratched his nose and gave me a direct stare as he asked, "How long d'you think you'll last?"

"Long enough," I replied, "to kick some butt. Do I need to start with yours?"

He looked away, inspected his fingers, replied in a muffled voice, "I doubt you'll last that long."

The place was beginning to fill up. A lot of disgruntled faces, some sleepy ones; it was midnight, time to talk to the troops.

Copp was in charge, yeah, but in charge of what?

Maybe he'd last the night.

Maybe not.

CHAPTER 3

THESE WERE MOSTLY YOUNG FACES HERE, as you would expect of any department undergoing rapid growth, and the mix was pretty good with minorities reasonably represented, including eight female officers. They were crowded into the overflowing squad room which had seats for less than half of them, the others layered along the walls on three sides in disgruntled anticipation of the midnight meeting with their new chief. The brass were characteristically huddled in the front corner to the right of the podium, captains and lieutenants with folded arms and blank faces determined to reveal nothing of what was going on in the gray matter behind them.

I spotted Sidewise and Taxidriver in a solemn group along the wall about halfway to the rear. Lila Boobs was not there when I opened the meeting but came in about halfway through, taking an inconspicuous position at the rear. Our eyes met briefly across that charged atmosphere and I was pleased to note some discomfiture there. She'd done something to the long blonde hair to make it appear much shorter and she was now wearing designer jeans and an oversize sweatshirt but there was no problem with the recognition.

I hit that group with both barrels, mincing no words and making no bid for popularity, wanting to wake them all up with a figurative slap in the face and inviting an angered reaction . . . but I got none. "Your town," I told them, "has become the laugher of the entire state, your politicians lampooned regularly in the Los Angeles *Times* and your bureaucrats ridiculed in Sacramento. And you people . . . you call yourselves cops? Your streets are totally out of control. Your citizens are terrified. The common street wisdom throughout this valley is that crime pays and pays big inside the Brighton city limits. Nobody respects you. Nobody likes you. Nobody feels comfortable with you people on the streets—nobody but the hoods and punks. You terrorize your own citizens who are jaywalking or driving a bit too fast but look the other way when the gangs swagger through. Cops? You call yourselves cops? There's a hell of a difference, you know, between a cop and a mere neighborhood bully."

I didn't want to give any comfort to the idea that I would be around short-term. So I told them, "Maybe I'm here today and gone tomorrow, and that's okay, maybe that's the way I'd prefer it, but I was brought here to kick butt and I want you to know that I am going to kick butt until someone takes me out. Who knows how many of you will still be here when that happens, or how many of those will have their same rank? I didn't bring a broom with me, people. I brought a baton as big as a baseball bat, and I'm going to lay it against the head of any officer who makes me feel disgraced by association."

I said a few other things, and I guess I scowled a lot and grimaced a lot—which didn't seem to matter much because not many were meeting my gaze anyway—and I ended the "get acquainted" meeting by telling them: "I'll be calling you in one by one for personal talks over the next few days. Meanwhile my office is open at any time to any who would like to initiate that talk. Now get out of here and go take charge of your city, but not until I get to the door. Each of you is going to look me in the eye before you get out of here."

And each one did. I even got a few smiles and here and there an enthusiastic handshake. One of the female cops even flirted with me. Not Lila Boobs, though. Turns out she is Detective Delilah Turner, Vice Squad. She gave me a cool, level stare as we shook hands. I told her, "You look better with your hair down."

She murmured, "Sorry 'bout that. I'll explain later."

"Can hardly wait," I replied, and went on to the next in line.

The brass were the last to leave, the three captains and six lieutenants. They'd remained near the podium in a huddle with a dozen or so other guys, including Sidewise and Taxidriver, until the line out was nearly exhausted, then all straggled forward as a group with the brass bringing up the rear.

Taxidriver was Detective James Manning, Burglary Detail, and Sidewise identified himself as Sergeant Grover Peterson, Investigations Unit. Both were grinning, maybe a bit self-consciously, so I grinned too and told them, "Joke's on you boys."

"Guess it is," said Peterson. "Or maybe it's on all of us."

"No, I think it's on us," Manning said with a chuckle. "Ice cream get home okay?"

"Hardly a drip," I replied, and went on to the brass. I closed the door on those guys and gave them a private ripping, told them, "You guys have been here through all of it. What the hell's the story? How'd it get so bad so quick?"

McGuire turned away from that one but another captain who identified himself as Roger Williamson badmouthed me right back. "If all you know is what you've read in the papers, then you don't know a God damned thing," he told me, but the tone was mild enough. "Maybe you should reserve your criticism until you get on board and see the problems up close. Hell, anybody can shoot a rabbit with a shotgun."

"Bullshit," said the other captain, a guy named Ralston. "Chief Murray was removed because he was flat on his ass and couldn't find the ground with either hand. I support everything you said, Copp. But I can't support you. You're no chief of police and you never will be."

"Correction," I said quietly, happy to have the honest feedback. "I *am* the chief of *this* department and I'll stay the chief until it becomes a real department. Test that, and you'll be on the sidewalk outside on your own ass before anyone can notice you're gone. You guys can think whatever you want to think, but you damn sure better toe the mark and take everything I say as gospel until some other chief comes along, otherwise you won't be here to greet him."

I addressed my final remarks to the lieutenants: "You guys be ready to fill vacant spots upwards or downwards, in case anyone is still wondering who's in charge here. Copp is in charge. He's going to shake this department out and stand it on its feet within seventy-two hours, and he's starting the shake at the top. So get ready for it."

I walked out, leaving some very sober faces behind in the squad room. Those guys all had my number, knew who I was and what I was about. And I could almost sympathize with them. I'd never risen above the rank of sergeant after fifteen years of public service, so who the hell was I to be reorganizing the entire police department of a midsize city? Worse than being a nobody, I was a failed cop in their eyes, a guy who could not or would not work within the system.

But, of course, that was the whole point of my being there. Carl Garcia knew my history, knew it well, knew me well enough to know that I had very little respect for the system that had produced this mess, well enough to know that I was not afraid of these guys *or* their system and that I would go straight for the jugular in dealing with the problems there.

I had a charter to kick ass.

That was exactly what I intended to do.

SHE WAS WAITING for me outside my office, sprawled in a chair at my secretary's desk and nervously twirling a stray lock of hair. She stood up quickly at my approach and tried a smile that did not quite work, told me in a husky voice, "I feel like such a fool."

I opened the door to my private office and ushered her inside, went in behind her and closed the door, waited until she'd settled into a chair in front of the desk before I went around and took my own chair. Hell, she was half a block away, on the other side of that massive desk, so I got up and went to the alcove, asked her, "Could you scare up some coffee?"

She murmured something and left with that same graceful stride I'd seen outside the supermarket earlier, returned a moment later with a steaming glass pot, took some cups off a sideboard in the alcove and poured the coffee.

"Sit down," I commanded gruffly.

She settled onto a chair at the opposite side of the alcove, tasted the brew, said, "Not bad for graveyard coffee."

"I always liked it the best," I told her. "Matter of fact, I always liked graveyard the best."

She wrinkled her nose in a smile that was genuine this time as she replied, "I have a hard time sleeping days."

"Me too. So I never slept much on graveyard."

We'd run quickly out of small talk. We stared at each other for a moment, then she said, "Uh... those guys recruited me for that little detail this afternoon under false pretenses. Said you were a smalltime private eye hired to poke around in the city's business. I—"

"Partly true. I am a private cop. But I have not been retained in that capacity."

She looked confused, but went on with her explanation. "Stings have become my specialty lately. Vice stings. We've been going for the Johns and seeing that their names are printed in the newspapers. Manning and Peterson approached me and asked for my help in setting up this private eye who had been hired to cause trouble for the department. Said they just wanted to roust the guy and give him some discouragement." She frowned. "I didn't much like the idea, but..."

"But you went along."

"I went along. I honestly believe that Manning and Peterson had been deceived too. They're good guys, good cops." She gave me an oblique smile. "Despite what you may have been led to believe, there are some good cops in this department."

I said, "Of course there are. Most are, I'd guess. The problem is at the top. Help me fix it?"

She squirmed briefly, replied, "I'd rather be a cheerleader than a player. I don't know from politics, don't know the game. I just want to be a good cop."

"Good cops," I reminded her, "don't look the other

way when shit is happening. They dispose of it. I can't do this job alone, Turner. Help me pick up the dog shit."

She stared gloomily into her coffee for a long moment then lifted troubled eyes to mine and said, "Okay. You can count on me. I'll do what I can. Just don't ask me to be a snitch, please. I have to work with these guys, maybe for the rest of my life. Don't ask me to..."

"I'm asking that you be a good cop. That's all. When you see shit going down..."

She showed me a sober smile, finished the statement for me. "Pick it up."

"Right. And deposit it here, in this office."

Something passed in our locked gazes, I don't know what it was but it was nice, and it was warm, and I liked it. Detective Turner set her coffee down and stood up. "Thanks for not holding this afternoon against me."

"I like you better with your hair down," I told her. "And, uh, I didn't mind what you held against me."

She actually blushed, started to say something but changed her mind and went on out. I followed her to the door just to see that walk again, but immediately the walk became a run and I joined it.

Two loud gunshots had come from directly outside, and everyone in there was running toward the sound.

Someone yelled, "Call the paramedics!" just as I stepped outside. There was a lot of confusion in the vehicle yard, uniformed cops milling about and a sergeant shouting orders.

Taxidriver and Sidewise were slumped in the same car they'd taken me for a ride in earlier.

Each had a bubbling bullet hole in the forehead.

Good cops? Maybe. Maybe not.

Dead cops, for sure.

The first bolt of lightning had struck already.

CHAPTER 4

THE DIFFERENCE CAN BE WAFER THIN between a good police department and a bad one, hardly noticeable at all from the outside because of the procedures and protocols that have evolved to produce the modern police machine. Even a terribly bad department can look like a good one if what you are looking at is the machine itself. If it's modern, it's a good machine.

This one was entirely modern, having been built almost entirely over the past decade with all the proper materials in place. It was not that these people did not know *how* to police; the problem was that they had lately lost the will to do so.

In the immediate aftermath of the execution-style slaying of two of its officers right outside its doors, this department at least momentarily regained that will, the machine hummed, and all the right things happened as if by magic. I was witness to admirable efficiency. The scene was secured, order restored and evidence preserved, the proper teams assembled and the investigation launched with all the smoothness I'd ever seen anywhere—and yet this was a department in shock. You could see it in the faces and feel it in the surrounding atmosphere as trained responses took over to guide stunned officers in their duties.

All that should have been done was being done, and well. This is the way it works when it's working right; there is nothing for a chief to do when all the Indians are doing their parts. Police chiefs are largely administrators, which is largely why I'd never had any ambition to run a department. I'm a cop and I always loved the work itself, not the administration of it.

I'm trying to explain why I was not directly involved in the official investigation of the murders on my front porch. The machine was humming, and there is no place in the machine for an administrator. I could see that it was humming and that the best thing for me to do was to stand clear and let it hum. I'd sized it all up in a single look anyway. The victims had been among the last to leave the midnight meeting. They were not on duty, not even assigned to the same units. The car in which they'd died was the only unofficial vehicle in the yard. It was Taxidriver's personal car, registered to him. The key was in the ignition, engine idling in parking gear. Each victim had been shot once in the head at close range.

My personal, snap conclusion was that they had been waiting out there for a third party when someone familiar and trusted had approached and fired without warning. Their weapons were undisturbed in their holsters and one of the detectives had been smoking a cigarette when he died. I could leave it to the machine to develop all the hard facts and work out an official theory of the crimes. What was left for me were gut feelings and a personal theory which I had to deal with by myself and for myself.

Possibly those guys had died as a direct result of the little roust they'd pulled on me earlier that day. I felt that I had to look at it that way. The machine itself would be looking at the alternative explanations: grudge killing, random violence, whatever. I was not there to solve incidental crimes; I was there to discover why the city of Brighton was falling apart, what was wrong inside the police department, and who would have reason to try to intimidate the new city administrator.

I figured that the best way to accomplish my personal objectives would be to follow up on the angle arising from the hostile actions by and against the two dead detectives. Who'd sicced them on me? Why? And were the answers related to their own deaths?

So I followed Detective Turner when she left there that night. What the hell, why not? She was the only visible link I had, and there was no compelling reason whatever to believe anything she'd told me during that interview in my office moments before her erstwhile partners were gunned down in the very shadow of that office.

There was another thought too.

Maybe she was in danger herself.

SHE WAS AN easy tail, driving a jeep-type vehicle with distinctive lights and high profile.

I was in the unmarked official car reserved for the chief and I kept well back, giving her plenty of play, secure in the idea that I could keep her in sight and well within closing range at that time of night without giving away the tail.

The older sections of Brighton have narrow, tree-lined streets with few thoroughfares and a stop sign at virtually every intersection, inspiring me to get almost too cute with my footwork. I started turning off the track to run a parallel street every other block or so, pacing my speed to hers and checking her through the intersections from the parallel course—which was okay except that I was not that familiar with the territory and we hit the big east-west boulevard, Foothill, which marks the beginning of the spread of the city into the higher elevations, while I was running parallel.

The street plan changes at that point so I could have lost her if she'd squirted across Foothill and into the maze of new development. The intersections up there are sometimes half a mile apart and separated by intricate patterns of odd-shaped subdivisions with circular streets and cul-de-sacs enough to drive you batty; you don't want to venture into those areas at night without a guide.

I got lucky. She'd pulled into a donut shop on Foothill. A police cruiser was parked there also, two uniformed officers were seated inside, and Turner was standing at the table conversing with them when I eased past.

I went on down to a 7-Eleven just beyond the donut shop and waited for her there. It was a short wait, only a couple of minutes, then she barreled east right past me along Foothill. Even at that time of night the traffic along that boulevard is respectable, which made it easier to tag closer to the jeep without fear of discovery.

Used to be, back before the freeways were built, that section of Foothill was the famous Route 66 immortalized in song, the main passage in and out of Los Angeles for folks back east wherever. Still has a few small motels and eateries but mostly now the old boulevard has been caught up in the development fever and offers an almost endless array of upscale shopping centers and other commercial establishments, glitzy restaurants, fast food joints, service stations and all the other requirements of a bustling population center.

Generally, the homes above Foothill are priced in the three to four hundred thousand dollar range, those south of the boulevard beginning to age and give way to apartment complexes and other lower-range alternatives which tend to present the larger police problem for such a city.

Brighton even has its own version of the *barrio*. It also has a redlight district, drive-by shootings—mostly the result of gang activity—and an adjacent unincorporated section where anything goes and usually does.

To the people located north of Foothill, though, all of that is out of sight and largely out of mind, and north is where most of the people and practically all of the influential people of Brighton live. A three hundred thousand dollar home can be hard to swing on a cop's salary, so I doubt that many of the cops in this town live north; I suspect that most of them live somewhere outside of Brighton.

I had no idea where Turner was leading me, of course, but I'd assumed that she was headed homeward and I wanted a look at where she lived and how she lived, so I was a bit surprised when she eventually swung north and began climbing into a ritzy area above Foothill. But now I had to lay back too much and play games with my headlamps, and I could not always keep her insight in the tumble of hills, curves, and switchbacks. Finally I lost her entirely, had to rely on my prowling instincts, found her car five minutes later tucked onto a hillside drive below a veritable mansion.

Forget three or four hundred thousand; this one was a cool mil at market bottom, and it was blazing with lights at two A.M. I knew she could not live there, unless Daddy was a millionaire. Looked like three levels of mostly glass front, overlooking the valley like some baronial estate, walled grounds with security decals on the gates and conspicuous Guard Dog warning signs. I jotted the address and cruised on by, parked around the next curve and hiked back for a closer look.

The jeep was parked outside the gates. There was also a pedestrian gate equipped with a CCTV-Intercom device. I kept out of camera range, couldn't see anything anyway. Wondered, too, about Guard Dog. Not for long. Didn't see him but heard his presence just beyond the gate, a deepthroated growling, then heard a handler shushing him.

I went on back to my car, turned around and re-parked where I could keep the driveway in view, waited. Again, not long. I'd been on the scene for about ten minutes when three quick gunshots broke the peace up there. Sounded like a handgun and almost certainly on the grounds, not within the mansion.

Before I could react, the jeep backed out of the drive and headed down the hill with its lights off. I went after it, heard yelling and cussing followed immediately by alarm sirens as I passed the driveway, turned on my headlamps then and tried to close on the jeep.

Didn't even find the jeep.

A police cruiser tore past me wailing and flashing as I approached the boulevard. Quick response. Turned on my radio, then, and tried to catch the play but there was no play. So I picked up the mike and checked in. "This is Copp. What's the play above Foothill?"

A female dispatcher responded, "Gunfire report, Chief, Ellenmount area. I've dispatched a patrol unit to check it out."

"Back 'em up," I ordered. "The disturbance is at 726 Craggy Lane."

"Got that," responded a cool male voice. "Unit four-oh-one responding."

"Beware of guard dog," I told him.

"Ten-four."

I waited while another unit was dispatched to the scene, then I requested a spot on the jeep, gave the license number. The dispatcher replied, "That's, uh, a restricted..."

I said, "Right. I just want a location spot."

Another car checked in: "She just passed me on Montezuma, headed into Helltown."

"Helltown?"

"Zone Four." the dispatcher explained.

Zone Four or Forty made no difference to me, I was a stranger in town, but you have to be careful what you say on a police radio these days. Anyway, I could guess about Helltown—a place where anything goes, and usually does, a place outside the jurisdiction of the Brighton PD.

I could leave it to the police machine to determine who had shot at what, and why. I wanted to know why Lila Boobs had run from that shooting and gone from the sublime to the ridiculous—the mountainside to the cesspool.

So I went to Helltown too.

CHAPTER 5

A CITY, YOU KNOW, is legally defined by its geographical boundaries as a political subdivision of a county, and a county is usually regarded as a political entity that is composed of cities, towns, villages and rural areas. The latter distinction does not always hold true, of course. The county of San Francisco, for example, contains nothing whatever outside the city of San Francisco. Some years back the city of Indianapolis extended its political boundaries to include the entire county of Marion and the two governments merged to form a single entity.

The Los Angeles metropolitan area involves more than thirteen million residents, no less than five counties, and hundreds of cities. I meet people all the time who do not know which county they live in, and there are even those who are confused about which city they live in. Some do not even live within a city and are not aware of that. There is a blending and homogeneity within this area that blurs political distinctions for those who are not politically minded, as well as for some who are very much so.

You can live in a highly developed section of Glendora, for example, that is almost indistinguishable from most other neighborhoods in that city—and your neighbor across the street is in the same neighborhood as you but he lives in Azusa, and most of the neighborhoods in Azusa are virtually indistinguishable from yours. You'll find in both towns the same names for theaters, supermarkets, drugstores, department stores, restaurants, and what have you. You will even find common streets which move serenely from city to city without changing names.

Start in Azusa on Foothill Boulevard and drive east to San Bernardino—a distance of some thirty-five miles—and you will pass through the cities of Glendora, San Dimas, La Verne, Pomona, Claremont, Upland, Rancho Cucamonga, Fontana and Rialto as well as Brighton without ever touching a rural area and with virtually the same street scene from beginning to end.

But you have passed through a lot of police jurisdictions and you have briefly encountered several unincorporated zones between cities, some in Los Angeles County and some in San Bernardino County. The unincorporated zones are policed—well, sort of—by the respective county sheriffs departments.

"Helltown" is one such zone, and it represents the worse result of conflicting political and jurisdictional responsibilities. None of the neighboring cities want any piece of Helltown, and of course Helltown does not desire any notice by those cities. There are no zoning or development restrictions, no police presence of any consequence, and of course no local government interference whatever. You can drive through Helltown in twenty seconds flat—it's just a narrow strip of boulevard separating two cities—or you could get stuck there for the rest of your life, which can be very short in that strip.

I'd never worked in this area—L.A. County ends at Claremont, a few miles west—but I'd spent off-duty time there now and then just to catch the color. There's plenty of color, if you don't care what you catch. It's a tumble of sleazy, room-by-the-hour motels, porno shops, saloons, nudie dives and liquor stores—yet the briskest business going down at any time of night or day is along the curbs and sidewalks where you can catch anything from rock cocaine to AIDS and syphilis without even getting out of your car.

All I wanted to catch, this time, was a gorgeous female vice cop who'd helped set me up for a fall even before I knew what I was falling into. And I caught her there, yeah, all the while wishing that I had not.

I LOOKED FOR the jeep and found her in a joint calling itself The Dee-light Zone, a whiskey and pizza emporium featuring topless (and largely bottomless) waitresses and two naked girls in a cage suspended above the bar who, one would have thought, were crazy in love with each other. I wondered how boring it must get for those kids to stand there and paw each other all night long, but they didn't seem to have reached that point yet.

There were other cages to the rear, bathed in flickering blue light and offering opportunities for patrons who could afford it and loved to be teased to "Cage Up" with a naked kid of their choice—the sex is facsimile rather than the real thing, but for some I guess it's sex enough for the moment. Joints like these learned long ago that they're better off policing themselves. House rules are usually strictly enforced by brawny bouncers with ever-watchful eyes and eager instincts, so the action usually stays within the legal limit.

Things were winding down in The Dee-light Zone when I got there, thanks to the two o'clock liquor curfew. Not even a joint like this one—especially a joint like this one—is willing to flout the liquor laws—because a suspended license is the quickest way to shut them down. So they typically announce a "last call" at the bar at about one-thirty. You can stack your drinks then if you want but it all has to be down the gullet by two, at which time all unfinished drinks are whisked away and you are stuck with non-alcoholic beverages and whatever food may be available, if the house remains open. This house never closed, it just shifted gears a bit during the dry hours.

So the bar was dry when I got there but the pizzas were still coming out of the kitchen. There was a sign behind the bar promising "Breakfast From 4 A.M." for the all-nighters and/or early risers, but no booze between two and six.

Place was still about half full, thirty to forty patrons, probably almost that many employees if you count bouncers and all. Seemed to be a hangout of sorts, much talk back and forth between tables as though everyone knew everyone else, and certainly the technically naked waitresses seemed at home and comfortable with the patrons, making a lot of eye and body contact whenever circumstances allowed.

Detective Turner sat in a booth along the back wall with a man of about fifty. Solid looking guy, casually dressed but very neat. They were sipping coffees and the conversation was very sober. I grabbed a chair and placed it at the end of their table, sat down with a smile, said, "Got here as fast as I could."

I could read nothing in Turner's face—not surprise, not joy, not sorrow, not anything. She was a total blank. The guy looked from her to me, put a spoon in his coffee and stirred it as he asked, "Who the hell are you?"

"Here, I'm nobody," I replied, still smiling. "Two blocks west I'm the chief of police."

He spilled it in two soft words, delivered without feeling: "Joe Copp."

"That's the one. Which one are you?"

He was a blank too. "I'm Tim Murray."

"*Ex*-chief of police," I acknowledged quietly, hoping my surprise wasn't showing.

He replied, "That's the one."

I looked at Turner. "That was a quick run from Craggy Lane."

I got a flare there. A nostril quivered as she replied, "What were you doing on Craggy Lane, Chief?"

"Keeping an eye on you," I told her soberly.

Another flare. "You were behind me?"

"All the way up, all the way down—yeah. Who fired those shots?"

"I did."

"Why?"

"Self-defense. I warned them, tie the dog or he's a dead dog."

"You were there in an official capacity?"

Thoughtful pause, then: "No."

"Want to tell me about it?"

"No."

I looked at Murray. "Do you know what we're talking about?"

He replied, "Craggy Lane, I'd say Harold Schwartzman's place." He smiled faintly at Turner. "You shot one of his Dobermans?"

37

She shrugged.

I asked Murray, "Who is Schwartzman?"

"Very rich man. Owns maybe half of Helltown. Owns this place. Owns me too, now, I guess. I run this place for him."

"Why?"

"Man has to eat, pay his bills. I didn't even get severance, not anything. Looks like I'll have some legal expenses coming up somewhere down the line. Couple of councilmen want blood from me."

"How much blood?"

"Enough that I'll need a damned good lawyer. Know one?"

"Don't you?"

He smiled, shook his head. "City Attorney always advised me."

"I hear he resigned. Over this?"

The ex-chief nodded. "A certain member of the council demanded that he bring criminal charges. City Attorney knew it was nothing but a vendetta. But the pressure was on and he refused to go along with it."

"Why the vendetta?"

"Couple of my officers busted this councilman's spoiled brat last year. Kid was dealing crack and dust in the high school. Father appealed to me, wanted us to look the other way. Couldn't do that. Got 'im off anyway. Bought himself a judge, I suspect."

"Which councilman is this?"

Murray sighed, played with his coffee, replied, "Look it up. You'll hear other things too. Don't believe it all. How long d'you think you'll last at that desk?"

"No longer than Monday," I admitted.

"Uh huh. So why'd you come?"

"I was asked to come."

"I'm asked to do lots of things. Doesn't mean I have to do them. Why'd you come?"

I showed him a faint smile. "Maybe I'm old-fashioned."

"That's what I figured. I've heard about you, Joe. Maybe too much. And maybe it's not all true. If I was you, I wouldn't wait 'til Monday."

"If I was you," I countered, "I wouldn't be running a dive in Helltown."

"Well . . . wait and see where you land, then make those decisions. I have kids in college. I have a mortgage, too damned many credit cards, and I have a wife who cannot tolerate public humiliation."

"But then you have Delilah," I suggested.

He frowned, and she glared, and I apologized. "Sorry. That's out of line. Even in a murder case."

"Who was murdered?"

I shot a quick glance at Turner, then said to Murray, "You didn't hear?"

He looked her way too. She told him, in a very small voice, "I hadn't gotten to that."

I told her, "It's the news of the night. Why hadn't you gotten to it?"

She said, "I'm not on duty right now, Chief, and I am not even in your jurisdiction right now. So why don't you save the interrogation until later?"

"That's not what I'd call it, Turner. What kind of cop are you? What kind of *woman*? You hightail it to Craggy Lane before there's time to get tags on the victims' toes, then shoot a dog and dash down here for smalltalk with your ex-boss—and that's why you hadn't gotten to it? Come on, give it a break! You're not on *duty*? The *hell* you're not on duty!"

"What's this all about?" Murray asked worriedly.

"I made a jerk out of myself this afternoon," Turner

39

told him in a voice trembling with suppressed rage. "Manning and Peterson set me up to help them discourage a certain private detective from nosing around the problems in Brighton. A few hours later I'm called in with the rest of the department to meet our new chief, and it's the same certain private detective we rousted. I tried to explain it but apparently he is a very unforgiving man and now he's trying to roust me back."

I said, "That's bullshit and you know it's bullshit. I'm not here to play games or footsies with you or anyone, and I didn't tail you tonight to embarrass or harass you. Has it occurred to you, Detective Turner, that the same shooter who found Manning and Peterson could be laying his sights on you too?"

She responded to that only with the eyes, and they seemed a bit squelched—maybe by fear or anxiety, maybe by something else.

Murray cried, "What are you saying? Manning and Peterson have been . . . ?"

"Yeah," I said soberly, "yeah, they have been. Who's next on the list? What the hell is going down here, Chief?"

It was like he hadn't heard me. "Oh my God," he groaned.

I asked, "Were the four of you involved in something?"

He responded to that one, raised his hand slightly above the head and made a sign in the air. A big, mean-looking Mexican was at my side instantly. Murray instructed him, "Show the gentleman where the door is, Billy."

I pushed Billy away and allowed him to see the immediate future in my eyes. "I know where it's at," I told him.

"*Show* the gentleman," from Murray.

Turner stirred and came to my defense. "I'll show him,"

she said quickly. She had to brush past me to get out of the booth.

Murray growled, "It's okay, Lila. Sit down."

She said, "No, I'll..."

We walked out arm in arm, and she whispered to me as we cleared the door, "Well, now that was really dumb!"

Maybe so, but it was only the beginning of dumb.

CHAPTER 6

RIGHT UP TO THE LAST MOMENT, there, I'd been developing a good feeling about Tim Murray. Now I wasn't so sure, and I wanted to talk to Detective Turner about that but she was not overly receptive to my conversation or to my presence in her off-duty life. "Let's find some quiet place to talk," I suggested as we walked through the parking lot outside The Dee-light Zone.

"I've got day shift tomorrow," she said pointedly. "Maybe *you* can function without sleep but everyone else can't."

"You've been doing okay so far," I reminded her, glancing at my watch. "Night's shot already anyway. Why did Murray throw me out?"

"Same reason as me, probably," she replied with a tired grimace. "I'm throwing you out too. It's a rule I have, Chief. I don't fraternize with the brass off-duty."

"You were fraternizing with Murray."

"Not exactly. The rule doesn't apply to him now anyway."

"What exactly, then?"

"What do you mean?"

"What was the nature of your business in there tonight?"

"I don't have to answer that. I'm not going to answer it. Goodnight, now. I'm going home."

I leaned into the car door to prevent her from opening it, said, "Murray seemed to take it hard, the news about Manning and Peterson."

"Why shouldn't he? They were his officers for quite a few years. What'd you expect, just laying it on him that way? I was about to tell him with some sensitivity when you came in and pre-empted me."

"I thought he overreacted."

"That's not how I saw it," she said. "Can I go home now?"

"You didn't come here just to tell him that," I decided. "You came for information *before* you laid it on him. Are you working homicide now, Detective?"

She just glared at me, said nothing.

"Is that also why you went to Schwartzman's home? What was his connection with the dead officers?"

She sighed heavily, showed me a defeated smile, replied, "Look, some strange things have been happening lately. I've been very confused about some of it. I'm just trying to sort it out, that's all. I'm still numb from . . . well, I knew those guys pretty well too. Chief Murray did not overreact to the news. They were good cops, maybe a bit flashy at times, but good cops and good friends."

"That's why you were so anxious to snitch on them."

It was like I'd slapped her. "That is a hell of a way to put it! What's to snitch? You knew who we were and you

44

knew what we'd done. I was just trying to give you some perspective."

"Thanks for the thought," I said drily. "I already had the perspective. Someone didn't want me coming to Brighton. Who? Why? That's what I need to know. Why should I be that much a threat to anyone? Can you give me that perspective, Turner?"

She was still hot under the collar but didn't seem to know exactly how to vent it. "Why the hell don't you just call me Lila, like everyone else?"

"Doesn't change the questions, kid," I replied.

"Doesn't change the answers either," she said. "Take your hand off the door, please. I really must go now. I log in at eight o'clock. Catch me then if you wish to continue this examination."

"What examination?" I growled, but I opened the car door and closed it behind her after she slid inside.

She lowered her window and said tightly, "Don't follow me, please."

"Lila Boobs," I said.

"What?"

"That's what I've been calling you to myself all night. So maybe it fits better than anything else, at least until you've leveled with me. We started off bad, kid. So let's forget the chiefs and Indians stuff, it never wore with me anyway, and I don't want it getting in the way of direct communications. Whatever game this is, it's being played for keeps. You go home and mourn your dead partners if you want to, but save a little grief for yourself too because you're in this thing as deep as they were and I don't think you're heavy enough to handle it alone. When that sinks in on you, give me a call."

"Where would I reach you?" she inquired soberly.

"I'll be camping in my office until they throw me out."

She smiled suddenly, a genuine smile, said, "Lila Boobs, huh?" and drove away.

I realized that it was the first real smile I'd seen on that pretty face. And I decided that maybe I'd gotten my message through to her.

I just hoped it wasn't too late.

It was, it seemed, a tad too late for me. Billy Boy and two of his pals emerged from the shadows of the building and leaned against my car, daring me to pass. I asked them, "You boys sure you want to play?"

Billy spoke for them. "Mr. Murray wants to make sure you get safely off the property. We just came out to make sure."

Sure they did.

I said, "Move away from the car."

"This your car?"

"Belongs to the City of Brighton. I'd hate to see it get dented by someone's head. So move away."

"City of Brighton's back there," Billy said, jerking his thumb in the wrong direction. "Sure you're not lost? We could help you find it."

"You'd better find yourself first, pal."

"I think you got a flat tire."

The guy was a prophet. I did not have a flat tire, until he said it. Then one of his pals produced a switchblade and very deliberately inserted it into the sidewall of a rear tire, all the while smiling at me with a self-satisfied leer.

I said, "Gee, I wish you hadn't done that," and then I kicked his balls into orbit while he was still bent over the wheel of the car. The leer turned abruptly into a very sick grimace and the guy fell over onto his side, moaning.

Life can be that way, you know. Go looking for trouble, you usually find it. I don't carry my black belt around with me, and I don't usually go around looking for someone to practice on...but it's okay, someone always comes looking for a go sooner or later, you just have to be patient.

Billy's other pal scooped up the switchblade and danced toward me in an improvised and badly executed Kung Fu shuffle, waving the knife in front of him like a Benihana chef as Billy himself warily circled the other way. I hit the chef with another kick at mid-shuffle. It caught him just the way I'd hoped it would, off balance and struggling with the choreography, sent him flying headlong against the building hard enough to rattle it.

Billy stopped circling, held both hands out at shoulder level and said, "Hey, wait, there's been a misunderstanding."

"I think so," I agreed.

"You have a spare?"

I threw him the keys. "Look and see."

The guy at the wall was lying in an unconscious heap. The other had begun to lose his stomach. Billy opened the trunk and looked inside, announced, "Oh yeah, right, we're in luck. I'll change it for you."

I said, "That's damn nice of you, Billy."

He huffed and puffed with the jack, changed the tire in what I would regard as record time, neatly stowed the flat and gently closed the trunk, laid the keys on it as he gave me a smile and said, "Good as new."

"Not quite," I corrected him. "Your pal owes the City of Brighton fifty bucks for a new tire. Can't patch a side-wall."

"That's right," Billy said agreeably, "you can't." He leaned over the groaning man and wrestled his wallet free, counted out forty dollars in fives and tens, added a ten from his own wallet and placed the wad under the keys. "There you go."

47

"Move the trash out of my way," I requested.

He said, "Oh, sure," and dragged the groaning man clear.

I claimed my keys and the fifty bucks, got in the car and got out of there.

Tim Murray was standing just outside the door to the club as I swung past. I waved at him. He waved back, but a bit uncertainly.

Why the hell, I wondered, had he put those guys on me? Not out of grief for Manning and Peterson, for sure.

So why?

The Copp in charge would need to find out why . . . and damned quick.

So I went straight back to 726 Craggy Lane.

CHAPTER 7

THOUGH I HAD BEEN ABSENT FOR NEARLY AN HOUR, I arrived back on the scene at 726 Craggy Lane in the midst of a growing police presence, which seemed a bit odd. A police line had been marked and the street secured a hundred or so yards south of the property, a half-dozen or so uniformed cops on hand and conducting activities on the street, two ambulances in the drive and a swarm of plainclothes cops on the floodlit grounds.

Pappy McGuire stepped forward to greet me. "Dispatch said you were on top of this," he complained. "Where've you been?"

"Out and about," I replied, still trying to get a feel for the situation. "Isn't this a heavy response for a dog?"

"I don't know what you're talking about," McGuire growled.

"So maybe I'm not on top of it. What's the story here?"

"They had a prowler. This joint is a fortress, you know, security devices all over the place. Also a twenty-four-hour guard force. One of the guards is dead."

I said, "Well, shit."

He said, "Shot three times in the chest. What were you saying about a dog?"

"I was told that a dog had been shot."

"You were told?"

"By the shooter." I told him the story, wondering how much of it he already knew anyway. It certainly was no secret that I'd requested a spot on Lila Turner's car moments after the shooting. Thinking back on it, though, it occurred to me then that Turner had not actually said that she'd shot a dog, not even in response to a direct question from Murray, she'd merely created the impression that she'd done so as an explanation of the shooting.

Now I had to wonder about it, and I said to McGuire, "Three bullets in the chest, eh?"

"Why would Turner tell you something like that?"

"You know her better than I do," I replied suggestively.

"Right, and I just can't hear her saying it. I also can't see her pumping three bullets into someone and then leaving the scene without calling it in. Anyone else hear this story?"

"Tim Murray heard it," I told him.

"What does Murray have to do with it?"

"I followed her to a joint in Helltown, the Delight Zone or whatever. Told me he's managing the place now. We sat and talked, the three of us. He heard the story just before he tossed me out."

"He tossed you out?"

"Symbolically, yeah. Turner walked me outside. I put her in her car and said goodnight. Said she was going home. Why don't you check that out?"

McGuire said, "Yeah..." and went off to find a telephone.

I nosed around and watched the homicide team at work, took a look at the victim, went back down by the vehicle gate to run some mental calculations, decided the timing was off a bit or else my memory of it was off. The body of the guard lay where it had fallen, twenty paces uprange toward the house from the gate, yet I'd heard Lila starting her jeep almost immediately after the shots sounded, hadn't even had time to get out of my car before she backed clear and went down the hill.

Time in the mind can be tricky. But if my memory of it was accurate, Turner would need to have been standing nearly alongside the jeep, which was outside the gate, when those shots were fired. And the angle was wrong for that. She could not have even seen the man from outside the gate.

The homicide lieutenant in charge at the scene, guy named Ramirez, told me that Schwartzman was not at home and that so far he'd not been located. Four domestic employees, all young women, lived in the house and were then being questioned by a member of the homicide team. A gardener lived in a cottage on the property, and he was being questioned. No one else was on the premises.

I asked about the dog.

Ramirez told me there were two dogs in a kennel near the gardener's cottage; both appeared hale and hearty, mean as hell.

No dead dog?

No dead dog, no.

I went inside the mansion, then, and took the measure of that. Some measure. Art treasures all over the place. Full-scale ballroom, complete with bar and bandstand, study, library, rec room—a kitchen capable of state banquets. Who was this guy Schwartzman? I'd never heard of him until that night. Upstairs and upstairs again were bedrooms all made up as master suites with Jacuzzis and the works.

I had no right to poke around that way, I knew it but did it anyway. Schwartzman's personal suite was fit for a monarch, his clothes closet as large as my own bedroom at home and I'd always prided myself on its size, maybe a hundred suits and that many pairs of shoes. In the midst of all that, the man slept in a waterbed—admittedly, though, a hell of a waterbed with a built-in footboard displaying a twenty-seven-inch combo TV/VCR and a library of videocassettes. Checked those out too. None were packaged products but had been labeled by hand. I tried one just for size and found that it met my expectations: amateur porn. Watched it for a minute, saw nothing recognizable except the action itself, which beat the hell out of some of the professional stuff I'd seen.

He had a cluttered desk in there, too, but I didn't even approach it, went on back downstairs and got in on the end of the interviews with the household staff. Two were Asian, one was Latino—the cook—and the other looked born and bred in Iowa or Minnesota, a chesty blonde, the kind who triggers male fantasies of being smothered in soft flesh. Turns out she was the housekeeper and personal secretary, and the only one of the four who spoke coherent English.

The story from inside fit, more or less. They'd heard gunfire and a car in the driveway. The alarms started ringing. The blonde dialed 911. That was it.

No, she had not heard any yelling or cussing immediately following the shooting.

No, there was but one security guard on duty at a time and all lived off the premises.

The gardener was Japanese and rarely left the property

except on weekends; he was "aged" and probably slept through the entire disturbance.

Mr. Schwartzman had not been home all day, and she did not know when to expect him.

Nothing appeared to be missing from the house.

That was it, in a nutshell.

Problem was, I was beginning to feel like the nut.

CAPTAIN MCGUIRE HAD been unable to locate Detective Turner at her home or at any of her alternate numbers. She had a widowed mother living in the area, a married sister, and a close female friend with whom she occasionally spent time; none had heard from her that night and none could offer a clue to her whereabouts.

I wanted to locate her, and quick, but I did not want to put out a formal APB, and McGuire agreed with that. Instead, we issued a soft watch and put a detective on the phone to call every cop on the force for information which could lead us to her.

"I don't believe she's running," McGuire insisted, "and I don't believe she's guilty of any misconduct."

"If you're right on both counts," I told him, "then it's even more important that we find her."

He gave me a searching look and asked, "How is that?"

"There's a pattern here, Pappy," I explained. "Turner was involved in some off-duty shenanigans with Manning and Peterson shortly before they were killed. I know she didn't pull the trigger on those two because she was at my side inside the building when they were shot. She came straight up here, though, spent about ten minutes inside these grounds, and left another dead man behind her when she left here. I found her minutes later in a sober conference with Murray. Why was your chief fired?"

53

McGuire looked at his feet as he replied, "Incompetence, they said."

"Was he incompetent?"

He looked at me then. "Aren't we all?"

"Now and then, sure," I replied. "How incompetent was he?"

"Enough to get himself canned, I guess."

"You supported the firing?"

"I was never asked."

"Suppose you'd been asked."

"Look, he just didn't grow with the department. I didn't support his promotion to lieutenant and I was mad as hell when they made him a captain. As for chief. . ."

"Then you did not protest the firing."

"Hell no, I did not."

"The other captains?"

"Relieved to see him go. Murray did not build this department, Copp. *We* built it. He merely kept out of our way, rubberstamped our recommendations, played politics for us. He was good at that."

"How so?"

"Part of the clique, the ruling clique. How do you think he became chief?"

"Tell me how."

McGuire seemed to be warming to the conversation, almost enjoying it. I saw a lot of bitterness surfacing there. "He and Harvey Katz—that was our esteemed mayor—were buddies, grew up here in Brighton together, were best buddies all through school. Katz was a jerk but he went into politics early, and I guess he was in a great position to capitalize on the growth of the city. His old man was a farmer, owned hundreds of acres close in to town, so Katz did well off the development boom. Meanwhile Murray had become a deputy sheriff, switched over to Brighton as a sergeant ten years ago—which, incidentally, was during Katz's first term as mayor. He—"

"You were here then?"

"Sure. So was Williamson, so was Ralston. All three of us were lieutenants then."

"And Murray was a newly made sergeant."

"Yeah." The captain shrugged. "Way it goes sometimes. What the hell, you can't fight city hall."

"When did all the city's political problems start?"

"Oh, hell, there have always been *problems*. But they began for Katz in a big way only a couple of years ago. He lost control of the city council, thanks mainly to the new voters who've been moving in steadily for ten years now. Couple of his buddies were voted out, and the new boys haven't always seen eye to eye with the mayor. Brighton is beginning to grow up, that's why all the trouble. I don't believe Katz would have been re-elected to another term."

"Has his killer been caught?"

"No, and probably won't. Some transient, we feel, an opportunistic robbery that turned into a killing. Don't quote me on this, Copp, but it was almost poetic justice for the guy to go that way. Did you know? He was with a cheap hooker in a by-the-hour motel room. The assailant apparently broke into the room, shot them both, took everything of value including Katz's car. The car was found abandoned up near Stockton several days later. A watch and a diamond ring Katz had been wearing turned up in a Sacramento pawn shop. It was almost poetic, yeah. Guy has a really nice wife, a class lady all the way, and two nice kids, and he spends his time with trash."

"It was a pattern, then?"

"Oh yeah," McGuire replied quickly. "It was definitely a pattern. He owned a couple of joints in Helltown, I understand, on the quiet."

That lifted my eyebrows. "Was he a friend of Schwartzman?"

"I wouldn't be surprised," said the captain.

I decided that neither would I. A pattern was forming, yeah. And I had to wonder if it was about to engulf Lila Turner—or if she was part of it herself.

I wondered, also, if it was engulfing me.

CHAPTER 8

MY FRIEND GARCIA, THE CITY ADMINISTRATOR, had likened me to a lightning rod, a device that is supposed to attract lightning and harmlessly ground it. I'd use a different metaphor for the present situation. Unless it was total coincidence, my presence in Brighton seemed to be having an opposite effect. Lightning was striking all around me, sure, but not harmlessly.

Just look at it. I'd been in charge for a matter of hours and already three people were dead. If it kept going at this rate, I could depopulate the town before the city council could can me.

I dropped by the newspaper office at four A.M. and went through their morgue of local news, thinking I'd better get a bit ahead of the game before it rolled over me. The guy at the night desk was very helpful, knew exactly where to go to bring the relevant past alive for me, and I learned a lot.

Learned, for example, when and how Mayor Katz had

Don Pendleton

lost control of his town. It was more or less as Pappy
McGuire had told me, but with a couple of details left out
of his account. The local police association, the cops'
union, had been instrumental in the balancing of the city
council, throwing their support to a couple of mavericks
who'd never been in politics before but won office a year
earlier on a reform platform. This in spite of the fact that
the police management group, usually influential in local
politics, had backed the incumbents.

The police association is not open to people in the management ranks, lieutenants and above, and the management group does not regard itself as a union, but usually
the two organizations work hand in glove when it comes
to political endorsements. The split during the last election
had left some wounds which, according to a recent newspaper article, were still festering.

The overall result, of course, was that the Brighton City
Council was now composed of two "reformers" and two
of the old guard who the reform slate had hoped to unseat.
In such a split, the mayor has the decisive vote. The mayor
was old guard, and he had narrowly squeaked out a re-
election.

Now, with the mayor dead, there was no decisive vote
and the council was deadlocked on virtually every issue
that came before it, neither side wishing to offer any sort
of strength to the other. Katz had been dead for only six
weeks but already the machinery of government was virtually frozen, and it would be another three months before
a special election could be held to fill the mayoral vacancy.

That was one problem.

Another problem had to do with the firing of the police
chief and city administrator, the resignation of the city
attorney, and the chaos in the police department.

In a singular show of unity, the council had voted unanimously to fire the police chief one week following the death of Mayor Katz. Apparently Murray had made enemies even among the old guard, and he no longer enjoyed the protection of his sponsor, the mayor. In a related issue, the city administrator was fired because of his opposition to Murray's firing, and the city attorney resigned a few days later in protest.

The editorial stance of the newspaper had been more or less neutral until very recently, when it began castigating both sides for the sorry state of local affairs. Much had been made of the sudden jump in the crime rate, relating this to the "morale problem" at the police department. A number of candidates for the chief's job had been interviewed and rejected during the five weeks since Murray was fired, and there had been vociferous controversy over attempts to appoint an acting chief from management, probably because all those guys had campaigned actively for the old guard, and the reform slate could not forget that.

Meanwhile there was also no city administrator and no city attorney. The hopelessly split council had lurched along like a rudderless ship until Garcia arrived and took over, just a few days before he contacted me. The editors wished him well but feared the worst: "Mr. Garcia has impeccable credentials for the difficult job ahead. Let us hope that sanity can triumph over factionalism within our city council, that reason can prevail, and that our elected officials will give the new administrator the cooperation required to get our city back on track. It should be noted here that two members of the council have given only contingent approval of Garcia's contract. Our advice, Mr. Garcia, is that you do not fully unpack your suitcase until all contingencies have been removed."

So my pal Garcia had walked into a hot one, made hotter

by a resentful element within the police department and, apparently, threats against his family if he stayed on the job. That last rang a bit close to the attempt to intimidate me even before I knew anything about the problem. I had to wonder about the stakes here. What exactly was everyone so lathered up about?

The man at the newspaper could not help me with that. Nor could he help me with information about Harold Schwartzman. "I've heard the name," he told me. "I think—isn't that the guy—came to town a few years ago and built the big mansion in the heights?"

That was the guy, yes, but my informant could add nothing to the identification. He even tried a computer search of the newspaper files but came up blank.

"I'd say the man avoids publicity," the editor declared.

I told him about the Helltown connection but even that failed to jog the memory, so I thanked him and went to work on the police file. It was really a mess, had been for several years, with charges of excessive force by arresting officers, repeated over and over, dereliction, corruption— name it, this paper had reported it—and a spate of lawsuits during the past year charging wrongful deaths and civil rights abuses.

I left the newspaper office with a troubled mind, but actually I hadn't gained a hell of a lot. I'd read a lot of the news articles before. It's not the kind of stuff that sticks in the mind if you have no personal interest. I'd known of the problems in Brighton, of course, but at a distance. Found myself wishing I was still at a distance.

The wish became sharply focused two steps outside the newspaper office. A car without lights lurched around the corner and climbed the curb trying to reach me, but the timing was bad. I jumped back into the doorway to the building and held my breath as the front end of the car scraped bricks on both sides of me. It careened back onto the street at full throttle and was half a block away before I could unholster my pistol, so I held my fire. Didn't get an ID on the license plate and I was not even sure about the make, model or color of the car. I did get a flash glimpse of the occupants, two dark looking guys of indeterminate age but probably fairly young and excited as hell with the game, and vaguely familiar. It was just a gut feeling, but a very strong one, that I'd seen those guys before—maybe at my midnight meeting at the PD.

If the gut was right, then the implications were ominous, to say the least. It was time to stop thinking in terms of resentments and intimidation, time to start believing in murderous intent directed at myself and a "game" of obviously high stakes. High enough to have produced three murders and an attempted murder—my own.

Time also, maybe, to re-think my own involvement in the mess. It was a game I could do without.

I just did not know how to quit it with my self-respect intact, however. So I headed back to Helltown, hopeful of finding a dark, four-door sedan with fresh scrape marks on the right front fender. If nothing turned up there, I'd roust the whole damned department again and search for familiar faces.

But I didn't make it back to Helltown that night. Neither did the dark sedan and, when I found it, mere scrapes on a fender had lost all significance.

I heard the report on my radio when I was only a few blocks removed from the newspaper office. A chase was in progress, two police units involved and a third closing on an intercept point. I could hear gunfire on the radio and feel the tension of the chase. So I took an intercept route also, missed the climax by about two ticks, arrived at the scene with the dark sedan rammed into the wall of an industrial building and ablaze. It blew just as I got there, and I could see the two men inside engulfed by the fireball, but they had not appeared to be struggling and I figured them already dead. The body of the car was riddled with bulletholes, most of the glass shot out. Six uniformed cops were standing nearby with weapons drawn, and I did not see a saddened face among them.

I saw elation, satisfaction.

It was the same car, yeah. But I felt no elation, no sense of satisfaction, and those two had just tried to kill me.

Something, yes, was very sour in the Brighton PD.

And now the death toll had risen to five. It would be revealed within hours that all five victims were, or had been, officers of the Brighton Police Department.

CHAPTER 9

IT IS ALWAYS DIFFICULT TO ASCERTAIN the true facts in a police shooting incident, even when all the evidence seems to point toward the use of excessive force—and then it's even more difficult. If you have an officer wounded in the fracas, then the scales automatically tip toward the cops. If not, then there is always the question of judgment and intent on the part of the officers involved in the shooting.

No reasonable person would expect a cop to shoot only when shot at; that is never the issue. An old maxim at police academies says that "he who shoots first, shoots last," and that is often the case in real situations. But an officer is supposed to be capable of exercising split-second judgment, to *know* in that split-second if his own life is or is not in danger, and to shoot only if it is. That is what all the training is about, and that is why we have shooting reviews every time an officer's gun is discharged. There are, unfortunately, some overly fearful cops who shoot reflexively in a confrontation which they perceive as dangerous, and sometimes it turns out that the victim was not even armed. More unfortunately—and much more rarely, I hope—there are still cops in this land who are willing and eager to shoot upon the slightest provocation, and who take the greatest satisfaction in doing so.

I offer all of this so it's clear that all of these thoughts were in my mind that morning in Brighton at the scene of the latest shooting. I knew it had been a "shooting chase" that produced the result because I had been running with my windows down and had heard the gunfire live as well as via the radio. I had also heard one officer report via radio during the chase that he was receiving gunfire, as a caution to the intercepting unit, and a variety of weapons were recovered from the burned-out vehicle.

But there was no damage to any of the police vehicles nor any other evidence that bullets had moved in both directions during the incident. By the time I had arrived within eyeball range it was all over. All I saw was the suspects seated upright in the crashed remains of the burning vehicle, neither resisting or struggling to get clear before the gas tank exploded, six gloating officers standing well clear with weapons still raised and ready—and I could not erase from my mind the feeling that those guys would have been giving one another victorious "high fives" if I had not been there.

The victims were burned beyond any attempt at recognition and it was some time before the wreckage had cooled enough for anything more than a cursory examination. The patrolmen involved were relieved on the spot and sent back to the PD to write their reports and prepare for a shooting review. The haggard looking homicide chief, Ramirez, took over at the scene. It had been quite a night for him. I hung around until the bodies were transported, then went to my office and crashed on the couch until eight o'clock, slept maybe two hours as my purchase on the oncoming day, showered and put on fresh clothing and had breakfast at a nearby McDonald's while going over a copy of the dispatcher's log for the night.

Saturdays are normally quiet at any PD, same as any other offices with a forty-hour work week. Brighton was no exception, even at such a strained time. I finished breakfast before nine and was going through the files in my office when a pleasingly attractive woman of about forty placed herself in my open doorway and greeted me. "Chief Copp?"

Dark hair cut close and curly, trim body, dressed casually in knee-length shorts and a clingy jersey blouse, sneakers—very pretty with intelligent eyes and expectant lips. "I'm Marilyn DiAngelo, your secretary."

I gave her a quick up and down, smiled, and replied, "Even on Saturday?"

"Do you need me? I just stopped by to . . ."

"How'd you know?"

"Grapevine." She had a very nice smile. "You're the talk of the town."

"Already?"

"Sounds like you had a crazy night."

"You heard about that too."

She came on in. We shook hands. I felt a bit awkward. Obviously, she had been Murray's secretary. I couldn't read happy or sad in her face, just nice. She told me, "I'd be glad to stay awhile and help you get settled."

"I probably won't be here long enough to get settled," I replied soberly. "But maybe you could help me onto a fingerhold. You worked for Tim Murray?"

She nodded. "The past five years. And I've been doing the necessary paperwork since he, uh, left."

"Did Murray get shafted?" I asked bluntly.

65

She met my gaze for an embarrassed moment, then dropped her eyes to say, "I never felt that he was incompetent."

"Get along well with him?"

"Well enough. He allowed me ... considerable freedom."

"Meaning that you ran this office for him."

She locked onto my gaze again as she replied, "That is what secretaries do."

I closed the file drawer and carried a stack of manila folders to the desk, deposited them there, told her, "From the looks of things here, you do it very well."

"Thank you."

"Thank *you*. Married?"

"Yes."

"Kids?"

"Two, a boy and a girl. They're in high school."

"Like your job?"

"I love my job."

"Do you live in Brighton?"

"Yes."

"What does your husband do?"

"He's a teacher."

"Treat you right?"

"When I treat him right, yes."

"So you've got it made."

She smiled, and it was nice—like the rest of her. "I guess so."

"You'd like to keep it that way."

"Of course."

"Do yourself a favor, then. You've been running this office for five years. That gives you a highly privileged view of this town and this department. Where is the garbage buried?"

The smile faded. "What?"

"Something stinks here. What stinks?"

She said, "I'm not sure I . . ."

"You do, you know what I mean. You have a stake in this town. Work here, live here, your kids growing up here. Where is the garbage buried?"

She had come in so perky, so composed, so nice. Now she was confused, troubled, unnerved. "I'd heard that you were very direct."

"Have to be. I'm in a revolving door. I'll be gone next week. You won't be. You live here, your family lives here. Give it a shot. Help me find the garbage."

She took a deep breath and showed me a shaky smile, then marched over to the file cabinet I'd just vacated, pulled open a drawer, removed a file, brought it to me and placed it in my hands, told me, "Maybe it's buried here," and left without saying goodbye.

I looked at the file, noted the tabbed inscription, *Task Force,* removed a single sheet of paper. It was a copy of a letter signed by Tim Murray and addressed jointly to the sheriff of San Bernardino County and the head of the regional DEA office, a notification that Brighton was withdrawing from the joint drug enforcement task force. The letter was dated three years ago.

While I was pondering that, Jack Ralston came into the office with a long face to tell me, "Maybe we have an ID on our two John Does." He placed two blackened badges on my desk. "Evidence technicians dug these out of the burned rubble of the car. Belonged to two of our undercover narcotics officers, Hanson and Rodriguez. Both men are missing, haven't been seen since early last evening." He sighed heavily, almost painfully. "There may have been a terrible mistake here."

I picked up the badges and inspected them closely. It

was obvious that they had been subjected to intense heat. I said, "Maybe. But I need to tell you something about that car and its occupants. Minutes before the car crashed and burned, it tried to run me down on the sidewalk outside the newspaper building. Obviously I had been under surveillance and the intent was to take me out. Do you still think it was your narcs?"

He replied, "All I know is that those were their badges. Formal identification is still pending. But if you're asking me what I *think*—well, yes, I think it's them."

"What about the vehicle ID?"

"No help there. Car was reported stolen just a few minutes before the patrolmen spotted it and gave chase. Why would anyone want to run you down? You just got here."

"I'm the type who makes enemies fast," I replied. "Or hadn't you noticed?"

The daywatch captain almost smiled, but it didn't quite get to the eyes before he switched it off. "Haven't noticed you making any friends," he observed sourly. "Heard you had a run-in with Tim Murray last night."

"Where'd you hear that?"

"It's still a small town, after all," Ralston said with a smirk. He collected the badges, went to the door, turned back to say, "I scheduled the shooting review for Monday."

"Reschedule it," I said. "I may not be here Monday. Two o'clock this afternoon."

Captain Ralston stared at me silently for a moment then turned and walked away.

I read the three-year-old letter again, returned it to its folder, and went looking for other tidbits from the files.

Found some.

Marilyn DiAngelo might have just been guessing . . . or she might have known much more than she wanted to know, was afraid of becoming involved in the politics that were tearing the town apart, and had genuinely tried to point the way for me toward the garbage. Whatever, it was more than a point, it was a shove—and I'd decided that Jack Ralston had been wrong about one thing, at least: I *had* found a friend in Brighton.

The tidbits I found in the files that morning were no more substantial than the lead the secretary had offered, but they gave me quivers and I've gone a long way on quivers many times.

I've said something already about the jumble of police jurisdictions in the area. That is always a problem, but local departments had joined with the counties years back to work out various reciprocal plans and programs leading to better law enforcement for all. One of those programs was a direct result of the all-out war against drugs. It involved the formation of a Drug Task Force composed of members of the various city and county police departments together with agents of the federal Drug Enforcement Agency, which allowed a regional and cooperative approach to the problem irrespective of individual police jurisdictions. The DTF for this area had been spectacularly successful.

So why had Brighton pulled out of it?

The tidbits supplied a possible explanation. They also supplied a tantalizing clue to where the garbage lay.

Have you ever heard that money stinks? In small piles it's hardly noticeable. But the odor from huge piles can become almost unbearable.

It can even carry the unmistakable smell of fermenting garbage when that is what it makes of men's lives. And sometimes it smells of death.

CHAPTER 10

IT WAS A MATTER OF RECORD that Brighton's participation in a number of large drug busts by the Valley Task Force had been crucial to the success of the operations, due largely to the fact that the busts had gone down inside Brighton itself and because the Brighton PD had actually initiated those investigations.

It was also in the record, however, that Brighton felt shorted in its share of proceeds from the cash and property confiscated in those busts. Typically, all proceeds are divided between the participating agencies in a complicated formula that is supposed to be fair and equitable, and such proceeds are supposed to be funneled right back into the war effort.

We are talking big bucks here. During the final year of Brighton's participation in the task force, the city received sixteen million dollars as its share of confiscations. Busts within Brighton alone that year yielded thirty-five million.

So Brighton pulled out and used the sixteen million to

fund its own strongly beefed up narcotics division.

That appeared to have been a mistake. Confiscations dropped during that first year to a little over five million, and held at about that figure over the two succeeding years. Apparently there had been some wrangling in the city council over the matter but Murray had stuck to his guns, the mayor backed him up, and Brighton remained alone in its solitary war against drugs. Surprisingly, drug arrests had climbed steadily during that period when confiscations were tailing off, but the busts were smaller and seemed to be largely confined to smalltime operators.

Occasionally during those years Brighton had cooperated with other agencies in the area and with the task force itself, but there had been no large scale regional operations out of the Brighton PD since their decision to go solo.

I asked Ralston about that and he referred me to Captain Williamson. "That's his headache," he said sourly.

So I called Williamson at home and asked him about it. I suspect he was drunk, or else I'd awakened him from a sound sleep and he's a slow awakener. The voice was furry and the speech slurred as he told me, "That was Tim Murray's pet project. I don't really know that much about it. I'm nominally in charge of that area of operations but I'm really not in that chain of command. Sergeant Boyd runs the undercover narcs and he reports directly to the chief, which we haven't had lately. Since you've become such great buddies with the ex-chief, why don't you ask him about it?"

"Who told you we've become great buddies?"

"It's a small town," he said, and hung up on me.

It was exactly the same comment Ralston had given me earlier. So I went over to the dispatcher and asked her, "Who gave the order to report my movements?"

That flustered her. She said, "I don't . . ."

I said, "Sure you do. Let me see the log."

She pulled a small clipboard from a pigeonhole near her console and handed it to me without a word. How cute. I'd been under surveillance since I left the PD following the shootings of Manning and Peterson, time in and time out at each stop of the night.

I returned the log to the dispatcher without comment, returned to my office and tried again to connect with Lila, struck out again at every number, decided to have it out with Ralston; called him in, closed the door, wiped the sour look off his face with a backhanded slap that put him on the couch.

He stayed there, gazing up at me with sheer hatred but wisely non-combative. "You can't get away with that," he growled.

"So file a complaint," I growled back. "Why was the narc unit hit?"

"Hit? It wasn't *hit*. Set up, maybe, with a stolen car. That's why the officers pursued, it'd just made the hot list. Terrible, terrible mistake."

"Try another," I insisted. "It was a *hit*. First me, then them. Maybe I can understand me. Them, I can't. Why them?"

"This is crazy," Ralston muttered.

I kicked at him, missed on purpose, told him, "Don't make me kick it out of you. You guys had me spotted all night. Every cop on duty knew exactly where I was at every minute. Why? What's so damned hot in this town? What are you guys covering? Not Murray. It can't be Murray." I kicked at him again, and this time I missed only a little.

He rolled off the couch and came up on one knee at the

wall, his service revolver in hand. "I won't take this shit, Copp," he said angrily. "Try that again and I'll take your leg off."

I turned my back on him and went to the door, opened it, turned back to tell him, "You're going to take a lot of shit, pal, before I bow out of here. If you guys think I'm going to roll over for you, think again. I've had cops like you for breakfast all my life and I'm starting to gag on it. Clean it up, starting right now. You won't enjoy it if I have to clean it up for you. Speaking of that, get ahold of Boyd. Do it now. I want him and his whole scruffy bunch in this office at one o'clock sharp—and I don't care where they are or what they're doing, I want them here at one."

I stepped outside and almost into the arms of a homicide detective. He pretended he hadn't heard my little speech to Ralston and I pretended I didn't see him until he spoke. "Chief, do you have a minute?"

I'd noticed the guy at the Craggy Lane scene during the investigation there, thought he was a sharp and on the ball, fairly young—maybe thirty or so. I took him by the arm and walked him toward the exit while we talked.

"What d'you have?"

"ID on the Craggy Lane victim—well, I mean, further ID."

"Yeah?"

"Yeah. Thought you'd want to know. He'd worked up there as a security guard since the place was built three years ago. There are three of them on rotating shifts. This guy was Franklin Jones. He used to be a K-9 deputy from the San Bernardino Sheriff's Department, expert dog handler."

"Yeah?"

"Yeah. He came over to Brighton when Murray did, ten years ago, got fired a few years later. But it seems that

he got the job with Schwartzman on Murray's recom-
mendation."

"Yeah?"

"Yeah. Isn't that strange? I helped ID five DOA's during
one watch and every one of them either worked or had
worked for this department. What is it?—open season on
Brighton cops?"

"Guess we're on a roll," I told him. "Thanks for the
info. Is the autopsy report in yet?—on Jones, I mean."

"Yeah. He got it three times in the heart. No way could
he have walked after that, his heart was totally mutilated.
Died on his feet before the fall."

"Recover the lead?"

"Bits and pieces. The shooter used frag rounds, explosives. Educated guess says they were .38 caliber or nine
millimeter rounds, but of course..."

We'd reached the exit and moved on outside to continue
the discussion. I realized I didn't know the officer's name;
told him, "Sorry—I forget your name. Too many too
quick last night."

He showed me a friendly smile. "Easy for me. You're
only the second chief I've ever known. I'm Tony Zarraza."

I asked him, "What kind of firearm do you carry,
Tony?"

He blinked and said, "I carry the official department
firearm."

I hauled out mine and checked it, a .38 Detective Special,
double-action revolver. "Just like this?"

"Yes sir. Chief Murray insisted that all plainclothes officers carry that piece."

"Patrol officers?"

"They carry Police Positives. No concealment problem
for them."

"Thirty-eights."

"Right."

I hefted the little pistol a couple times as I asked Zarraza, "Vice officers carry these pieces?"

"If you mean Detective Turner, yes sir, she carries the standard piece."

"What killed Manning and Peterson?"

"Thirty-eight jacketed hollow-points."

"The two narcs?"

"Same type, yes. I meant to tell you, the fire did not kill them. Both were shot to death. Explosion had nothing to do with it."

I tisk-tisked and said, "Bizarre incident, huh. You seem like a sharp cop. Why do you suppose those two were in that car, at that place, and at that time?"

"Narcs are a different breed," he told me. "Every one's a cowboy. I have no explanation."

"What would you say if I told you that those two tried to run me down with that car moments before they got it themselves?"

"Are you telling me that?" he asked quietly.

"Yeah."

"Then I would say off the cuff that they copped the car for a hit and couldn't afford to be stopped in that car."

I said, "Yeah, I had it doped that way too. But now I'm wondering . . ."

"Sir?"

"Are you aware that I have been under official surveillance since I got here last night?"

"No sir, I didn't know that."

"They've been keeping a log on me at Dispatch, every movement, every stop, every start. Why would someone want that?"

Zarraza looked around a bit nervously as he replied, "There are some here, Chief, with fierce loyalty for Chief

Murray, who think maybe there's a chance he'll be reinstated. I think they're scared to death that your appointment might stick."

I said, "I think it's more than that. I think there's some heavy garbage buried within this department, and I think a lot of someones are scared to death that I'm going to sniff it out."

He said, "Now that you mention it . . ."

"Yeah?"

"I think you're right. I've caught the whiff myself, now and then."

I said, "Thanks for leveling with me, Tony. I don't know what it will cost you in the long run, but . . . thanks, I appreciate it."

He smiled and replied, "Hey, I just try to do my job." He looked about him, lowered his voice to add, "But thanks, I'll keep the eyes and nose open."

"That would be wise," I said, and went on down the steps toward my car.

He came down behind me, called to me, said, "I had the feeling you were going to tell me more about the narcs."

I looked him up and down, asked him, "Think you can handle it?"

"I'm willing to try."

"I believe that one or more of those patrol officers this morning were ordered to hit those guys, one way or another. Maybe it was set up that way and maybe it simply fell in that way . . . but I think it was a hit, sure and certain, and I think the order went down before anyone knew that the hit on me had failed."

That shocked him. "You're really serious about this, aren't you?"

"Well, I don't want to get *dead* serious," I told him.

"I've been working with these people for more than three years. I find it hard to believe that . . ."

"You've been a cop for more than three years," I guessed out loud.

He nodded. "Worked back east for awhile. My wife loves California, so . . ."

"You know how the mob does it, then. They hire the hit then hit the hitter. It's cleaner that way."

"You're not saying that the mob is behind this."

"Not that mob," I replied. "But every town has its counterparts. I think we could have a mob here, yeah, right in this department."

"I'd rather not believe that."

"Don't believe it, then, but open the eyes in the back of your head, too, if you're not one of them—and especially if you *are* one of them. There's a death squad in this department, Zarraza. And right now it's on a rampage."

He said tightly, "Thanks, I'll keep it in mind."

"Do that," I said, and then I went to find Tim Murray again.

The thing was closing in on me. I felt it in the bones, and I felt it in other people's bones too. Had to keep pushing, keep the pressure on. And then hope that I'd be standing in the right place when the bubble burst. Trouble was, as it turned out, the bubble was really a powderkeg, and there would be no "right place" for anyone to stand.

Already five were dead.

And I'd been in charge for only one night. How many more could I last?

CHAPTER 11

MAYBE I SHOULD REMIND YOU ONCE AGAIN that this was a police department in shock. It gets bad enough when a single officer is slain; it disturbs the equilibrium, reminds these guys that they are mortal, after all, and involved in highly hazardous work. It shakes up the wives and girl friends, frightens the kids, and invades the dreams of everyone affected. Here, we had four dead cops and an apparently related killing of an ex-cop. You didn't see tears or that many long faces around the department but this was symptomatic of the shock itself; what you saw was precision drill and machine efficiency in the daily routines, all imbedded in a palpable atmosphere of gloom approaching despair. It was as though the killings were the final straw for an organization already reeling and going down for the count.

I was a factor in that atmosphere, of course. I knew it. But I did not know how to become a positive factor except by accomplishing the task I'd been hired to perform. *Kick some butt* was my charge from the official who hired me. *Find the garbage. Dispose of it.* I did not see how I could do that, however, without broadening the jurisdiction to include the entire city government, because I felt instinctively that the problems had begun in that broader arena and would have to be addressed there, as well.

Problem was, I didn't really know where to start. I'm no whiz kid, I'm a cop. Despite what you might have seen on television, police work is generally a drudgery, not a drama—and although the TV cops always seem to wrap a case during their twenty-two-minute time slot on the tube, it takes longer than that to write up a report in the real world. Give me six months and a couple of dedicated spirit guides, maybe I could root out the problems in this department and restore its self-respect—but, a couple of *days*? No way, and I knew there was no way.

I could not deal with the problems because I could not find the problems within such a brief time frame. I knew that up front, and I believe that Carl Garcia knew it too. When he referred to me as a "lightning rod" I believe he was acknowledging that understanding. He expected the problems to come to me.

And apparently they had.

I could deal with problems that came to me, or at least I could try, and I had to see it as a blessing.

He'd hired me as a catalyst.

So, okay, I'd been catalyzing. And five were dead.

MURRAYS HOME WAS in one of the more "mature" neighborhoods north of Foothill, meaning it was among the first to be developed in the extended areas of Brighton. It was a nice, traditional ranch style on a large corner lot, three-car garage, manicured lawns and flower beds, a basketball hoop on the garage and a pool in back. I knew what his legitimate income had been because I was hired in at the same salary with a daily bonus "ride" in recognition of an expected brief stay. I could not say that he appeared to be living beyond his means, especially since he'd been in the home for nearly ten years; he'd bought in a lot cheaper than you could today.

A very pretty woman answered my ring. She wore a tennis outfit and appeared to be preparing to leave when I arrived—garage was open and a door stood open on the only car inside, an older station wagon.

I introduced myself and we shook hands while she introduced herself. Murray's wife. That surprised me, because this woman at first glance appeared to be about thirty years old. Murray was easily fifty. If she was anywhere near that then she was remarkably well preserved.

"I just got home," she informed me. "Let me go see if Tim is awake."

It was a few minutes past ten. She hadn't invited me inside so I stood in the open doorway and waited, but it was not a long wait. Mrs. Murray was back almost immediately, told me: "Gosh, I guess he didn't get home yet. I'm sorry. He—I just assumed—I have early tennis on Saturday mornings. I assumed he was home when I left."

"Assumed?"

"Well, he—we have separate bedrooms. Because of his hours now. He usually gets home around four o'clock and I'm a very light sleeper. So..."

"I understand," I told her, understanding maybe more than I had a right to. When a marriage is good, any time to get home is a good time, but not to a cold bed. I angled a look toward the garage. "You must have been in a hurry this morning, didn't even notice that his car wasn't in the garage. Or maybe it was."

She gave me a surprised look. "You know, I don't know . . . I *was* running a little late. I just don't know." She brightened. "Oh, shoot. That's why. He hasn't been using the garage. The door is so noisy. Wakes me up every time."

"He would have parked on the drive, then."

"Yes. You know, I just didn't notice. Isn't that funny?"

Me, I thought it was tragic. I asked her, "Do you have any idea where I might find him?"

"Did you try the club? Sometimes he works out. Or you might try the mansion."

"Which mansion is that?"

"Oh, I—" She giggled. "I assumed you knew." She assumed a lot. "The Schwartzman mansion? Up the hill?"

I thanked her and took my leave, but she followed several steps along the walkway and asked me, with a trace of embarrassment, "Have you met Lydia Whiteside?"

I turned and showed her a sober smile, replied, "I'm not sure I . . ."

"She's the housekeeper up at the mansion. I'm told she's very beautiful."

I smiled on as I told her, "Well . . . depends on the taste. Me, I'd take you."

That really flustered her. She said, "No, I—I was just—have you replaced Tim permanently?"

I said, "I think I'm just the relief man."

Mrs. Murray was visibly pleased to hear that. "We'll get this straightened out," she assured me. "Tim will be fully vindicated. They'll see."

I said, "Gee, I hope so," and went on to my car.

But I didn't think so.

* * *

I WAS MET at the pedestrian gate by a man and a dog. The dog seemed okay. The man didn't. "What'd you want?" he growled.

"Harold Schwartzman," I said.

"Who?"

"Schwartzman? The man who lives here?"

The guy said, "Oh, he's not here."

I showed my badge through the iron bars and told him, "I'll just come on in anyway."

"Well, I don't know. I better call the house and ask. Just a minute."

The guy disappeared from view. The dog didn't, but seemed friendly enough. I said, "Good doggy," and he wagged his tail in response, what tail there was. Magnificent Doberman. I'd seen him earlier in his kennel, or one just like him. I could hear the man talking offstage, evidently through a call box, because I heard a responding female voice say, "Let him in."

"Open the vehicle gate," I instructed the guard. "I'll drive in." I went back to my car, the gate opened magically, I drove in.

The drive circles uphill and takes you to the front door beneath a portico. Nice grounds in daylight, heavily planted in flowering shrubs and young trees. I saw a tennis court that I had not noticed on the previous visit, a pool with several cabanas. It was a good day for a view, the air crisp and clean, not even any smog shrouding the valleys. I could see San Bernardino, probably Riverside and the sprawl southward toward San Diego, most of the valley towns westward as far as Pomona, Mt. Baldy behind me and the peaks of San Gorgonio to the east. Great spot.

I left the car under the portico. An Asian girl with scared

eyes opened to my ring and escorted me to the chesty blonde, who was having coffee at a sunlit window table off the kitchen. I confirmed that she was indeed Lydia Whiteside, then I introduced myself. She poured coffee for me. We got friendly.

"I saw you last night," she reminded me.

"Saw you too," I assured her. In a somewhat different light, though. She'd looked like a kid last night, in pajamas and dressing gown. The sunlight showed her older, maybe thirty, maybe more, but no less attractive. She, too, was in a tennis outfit. I asked her, "You didn't just have a match with Mrs. Murray, did you?"

"Tim Murray's wife?" She laughed. "Hardly."

"Why hardly?"

She got serious. "I'm out of her class. What can I do for you, Chief?"

I carefully sipped the hot coffee and told her, "Just trying to get a feel for things. I'm new here."

"I know. What kind of feel did you have in mind?"

That was an open flirtation. I wasn't expecting it so I flubbed it. "How well do you know Tim Murray?"

"He works for Mr. Schwartzman now," she replied, taking my size with her eyes. "What do you want to know?"

"Where is Schwartzman?"

"He's out of town."

"That wasn't the story a few hours ago. You said he hadn't come home."

"Still hasn't," she said, grinning. "Sometimes he doesn't come home for weeks on end. Is that a crime?"

"Not as far as I know," I said, "but it could be a wonderment. Where does he spend all his time?"

"Depends on what he's got in mind," she said, getting flirty again.

I said, "I believe you're being evasive."

She said, "I believe you're being a cop."

"That's what I get paid for."

"All work and no play . . ."

"Bingo," I said, "that's my number. I'll play later. Right now I'm working."

"I'll play with you."

"Okay." I took a tall pull at the coffee. "I'll let you know when. Right now, can we work?"

"You're a very attractive man."

I said, "Thanks, you're a very attractive woman. Where can I get in touch with Schwartzman?"

"I thought you were wondering about Tim Murray."

"Him too. One at a time, huh? Schwartzman first."

"Mr. Schwartzman is a business man, a very busy business man. His business involves travel. He does not usually give me a copy of his itinerary, so I don't know where you can get in touch with him. When he calls in, I'll tell him of your interest."

"Does he call in often?"

"Depends."

I said, "Uh huh. What kind of business is he in, other than the joints in Helltown?"

"I'm not exactly sure," she replied with a straight face. "I think mostly, though, it's properties. And finance."

"What do you do for him?"

"I thought we covered that last night. I run this house for him. And his office."

"Can I see the office?"

"You're in it," she said, smiling.

"That informal, huh?"

"Mr. Schwartzman is the soul of informality."

I said, "I'll bet. Can I go upstairs?"

"Why?"

"I'm looking for Tim Murray."

"Here? He doesn't live here. But I'll take you upstairs if you want me to."

"What would we do up there, without Murray?"

She shrugged, grinned. "Whatever you had in mind. We could watch TV. There are some great tapes up there."

I said, "I sampled a couple last night while I was here."

"Oh, that's naughty," she said. "You should never watch tapes like those all by yourself."

I said, "With someone else, why watch tapes? I'd rather make my own."

Her eyes did that coy thing that only female eyes can do as she told me, "Okay, we could do that."

"But that would be part of playtime," I said regretfully, "unless . . . that's not part of your employer's business interests, is it?"

She laughed teasingly and said, "Gosh, you do love to play cop, don't you?"

"Five people were killed last night," I said. "That's not playing."

Her eyes jerked a bit. "*Five* people?"

I read the roster of the recently dead from memory, then asked her, "Did you know any of those people?"

She said, "No, I—just Frank Jones. But . . . what's going on?"

"How well did you know Jones?"

"Not well. He's worked here for years, but I didn't see that much of him . . . My God!—are you saying that they were all connected?"

"Yeah. That's what I'm saying. And I suspect they were all connected to your boss." I stood up. "I really need to talk to him. Tell him for me, won't you?"

She was still *my Godding* as I let myself out.

I retrieved my car and rolled back down the hill toward Helltown.

I would have loved to have stayed and played.

CHAPTER 12

HELLTOWN LOOKS DIFFERENT BY DAYLIGHT TOO. Take away the neon surface and what's left is aging and neglected buildings, dirty streets and cracked sidewalks, a general ambience of decay. It even smells different by daylight.

But that did not seem to keep anyone away.

The whole boulevard was bustling with activities which only looked different by daylight. The hookers, the dealers, the johns and the jerks did not need the cloak of darkness here for a sense of security; their security came with the territory. Maybe a listless sweep by a sheriff's squad once or twice a month just to feed the myth that the strip was being policed—an occasional item for the newspapers, couple of small drug busts, a hooker or two slapped on the wrists—that was about the extent of official police presence here.

Ah, politics—and the price we the people pay for the illusion that we are in charge of our government. The politicians are in charge, folks—the politicians—and don't

89

ever forget it. Show me one who is living entirely off his official salary for "public service" and I'll show you a guy who has not yet learned the ropes. Give 'im time, just give 'im time, and he'll soon be as big a whore as any, lying down for anyone when the price is right.

And it's not just our elected officials who see "service" as a one way street leading only to themselves. Look at your bureaucrats too, look—no, don't let me get started, I'll talk all day, and talk means nothing. Throw out one bunch of crooks and you merely open the doors to another. We can't talk our way out of this problem, can't bitch it away; we're stuck with it because we created it—and some very wise man a few thousand years ago told it the way it is: a people have the government they deserve.

If I sound cynical it's because I've been a garbage man all my life, and people who deal with garbage all the time stop believing the illusion.

While I'm on the subject, though, you want to hear something cute? A day has not gone by for months when there has not been a news item buried in the interior of the local newspapers or given a two-second blurb on television mentioning that another innocent child has been gunned down on some neighborhood street or while playing in his yard or sleeping in his own bed. It has become such a routine event that it is no longer regarded as hot news. The news people report it almost as an obligation, usually under the heading of "another drive-by shooting."

What is this shit? It's a crowd of hyped-up, drugged-out, fucked-up, soul-dead moral midgets drawn together as juvenile street gangs who think it makes a big man to pull a trigger on a two-year-old child asleep in his crib. These are gangs that can't live straight, can't think straight, and can't even shoot straight; they're killing everyone except the people they're shooting at. The gag is this: you pile three or four jerks just like yourself into a car, give everybody a gun that doesn't have to be aimed—just point it and pull the trigger, you're bound to hit something besides air—and drive through a neighborhood that is not your own. Then you pull the triggers any time you see something move. If you don't see anything move, pull the triggers anyway—what the hell, you came down here to pull triggers, didn't you?

What has happened to public outrage? Why hasn't the national guard been activated by the governor to go into these neighborhoods and round up these jerks, throw them in a bag, and toss it in the ocean? Know why? Because they're mostly juveniles, and we don't treat juveniles that way nowadays. We send them to school. They get out of school, go back to their neighborhood, and start cruising other neighborhoods again. There are more out of school than we can ever get into school, so it's a revolving door and a losing battle—and, before you know it, you've got brigades of adult jerks who've learned all the wrong lessons in the right place, and the cycle continues.

Know what's cute? Nobody gives a shit. That's why you don't see screaming headlines and outraged bulletins on the TV. Nobody gives a shit.

Interested in knowing what happened to public outrage? Look at what *is* news. Protest marches on abortion clinics, debates on the environment, obscenity trials, political scandals and campaigns, white collar crimes, anti-smoking crusades, the drug wars.

Jesus.

Where has our outrage gone? It has gone to the minor issues, pal, and we've all been seduced by the illusion. Murder of children in the streets is not nearly as outrageous as cigarette smoke in a restaurant or cruelty to animals, not in this America.

91

Do we have the government we deserve?

Well, I don't know about you, but the folks along the Helltown strip certainly had the government they wanted. Don't wonder why a cop gets cynical. He's cynical because he knows where your interests lie, and they always seem to lie in the wrong places. As long as little kids are being murdered in their beds with no public outcry, don't blame a cop for being just like you. I'm talking about *self*-interest, yeah.

At bottom, the folks at Helltown are no different than you. Their self-interest is merely directed into different channels than maybe you would have, but the focus is the same.

I had all this shit going through my head when I walked into The Dee-light Zone that Saturday morning. It was about eleven o'clock and the joint was at full blast. I didn't see Billy Boy but a couple just like him sized me as I walked in, then turned away and allowed me to find my own way inside.

I found elbow room at the bar and cased the place while waiting for a bartender to notice me. Saw no one familiar, place was filled up and cooking, waitresses jiggling around with trays of drinks and rowdy patrons going for free feelies when the bouncers weren't looking their way. There were female patrons here and there, also, and you could easily identify them without a program: a few butches, a few hookers, an obviously "tourist" group of mixed sexes who were there just to sample the atmosphere.

About a foot above my head and no more than an arm's length removed, the gilded cage rocked with the energetic movements of two naked Mexican girls with long black hair and oiled bodies who were engaged in a simulated wrestling match, though it really did not look like that. Each seemed to be struggling for a leglock on the other's head but the oil was making it difficult. Noise level in there was almost dizzying, and the guys around me at the bar were adding to that as they egged the girls on: "Bite 'er clit, Lola"—"Get 'er by the short hairs, Izzy!"

I have to admit that there's something about the sight of two pretty girls going at each other that way that turns most men on. I don't pretend to understand it even though I'm affected by it myself; most of those guys in there would have puked or thrown something at the cage if it'd been naked guys slithering around together in there—outraged, yeah.

Speaking of which, a bartender finally found his way to me and asked, "What's your pleasure?"

"Someone just got killed," I told him glumly.

"Yeah? Who?"

"Some little kid, don't know his name. Drive-by shooting victim."

The bartender said, "Oh, that. What're you drinking?"
Oh, that, sure.

"I'm not drinking. Looking for Tim Murray. He around?"

The bartender wrinkled his forehead. "Tim? Naw, I'm sure he's not. He comes in about two, usually. Anyone else? Looking for a job?"

I said, "I got a job. Who's in charge right now?"

"That'd be Vic." He pointed toward another bartender at the far end of the bar. "Hey, I got drinks cooking. Catch ya."

I went to the other end of the bar and stepped behind it. "Vic" gave me a quick, questioning look and moved toward me. "Stay on the other side of the bar, please," he said in a no-nonsense tone.

I stood my ground and told him, "Can't reach you from that side. I'm Joe Copp. Looking for Tim Murray."

93

He said, "I don't care if you're Alley Oop, you can't come behind the bar. Step back out, please."

So I stepped back, told him, "At least I got your attention. It's important. Where can I find Murray?"

"We're very busy."

"I can see that. Tim won't like it when he finds out you gave me a bad time. This is for him, not for me."

"Are you a cop?"

I nodded my head and showed the ID. "Tim's replacement."

Vic said, "Oh, well."

I tried to look as friendly as possible under the circumstances. "One more time, pal. Where do I find him?"

"Find a table, why don't you? I'll try to reach him."

I said okay and went looking for a table. One of the jigglers grabbed me and steered me to a booth in the rear, behind the other cages. I'd seen Vic give her a high sign just before she closed on me, so figured he'd know where to look for me. The girl massaged my shoulder as she sat me down and asked, "What can I get you?"

"Coffee," I replied.

"Nothing in it?"

"Just coffee."

She smiled and swayed away. Before I could get settled, another came along and moved on me with a seductive smile, a goodlooking brunette with hair to her hips and not much else for concealment. She slid into the booth and leaned into me, one hand rubbing my leg just below the hip, and said, "Hi, honey, I'm Sandra."

I said, "Hi, Sandra—get lost, Sandra. I'm here on business."

The smile vanished with a crash and she replied, "Oh! Well, they put you—okay, I thought you were here to cage up. No big deal." She slid out and strode away with an angry bounce.

The other girl came back with my coffee and set it down without a word. She was going to leave that way but I called her back. "Worked here long?"

"Too long," she replied warily. "Vic told me who you are so please don't try to be funny."

"I'm not feeling especially funny," I told her. "Four of my people were killed last night."

She said, "Yes, I heard it on the news this morning driving in."

"Did you know any of those guys?"

"I don't think so. A lot of the Brighton cops come in here when they're not on duty. But I don't much know for names. Please, I can't stand here and talk to you like this."

"Just one more. Do you know Tim Murray?"

"He's my boss, now. Sure, I know him."

"Did he come in here much while he was chief at Brighton?"

She wrinkled her nose. "You're trying to get me in trouble."

I held up both hands, smiled, told her, "No way, kid. This isn't my territory."

She said, "I know," and looked toward the bar. Then she turned back to me and added, "I think Tim Murray got shafted. He used to come in here as a customer now and then, sure, but he was always a gentleman and he still is a gentleman."

"Was he here when you came to work today?"

"No." Another glance toward the bar. A bouncer was coming our way. "His car is here, though. It's the gold Chrysler parked in back in the reserved slot. I have to go."

She went, opposite to the approach of the bouncer. He leaned over the booth to tell me, "Vic says he can't find him. Sorry. But the drinks are on the house. Stay as long as you like. Want me to send a girl over?"

I said, "No, thanks," and the guy smiled at me and went away.

If the drinks—and maybe some other things—were always on the house, maybe I knew why Brighton cops liked the place. Of course there was nothing irregular about that. Even the doughnut shops give freebies just to have cops around during the haunting hours.

I finished my coffee and went on out, walked to the back of the lot and found the area reserved for employee parking, spotted the gold Chrysler. It was one of the small ones, convertible, sort of sporty, a bit out of character for a public official. So maybe it was brand new, bought from the proceeds of public service after the service had ended.

The door opened to my touch. Keys were in the ignition. I just had a feeling, took the keys and went to the trunk, opened it.

I don't know, maybe I smelled it.

But I knew what I would find in that trunk.

He'd been dead long enough to go stiff.

I closed the trunk, returned the keys to the ignition, and went quietly away from there.

This murder would make the headlines, sure. But for all the wrong reasons. And business in Helltown would go on as usual, that much you could bank. Tomorrow's headlines would be concerned with the budget crisis in Washington, or maybe what one gubernatorial candidate said about another. People in this country are no longer outraged by the truly outrageous.

CHAPTER 13

I CALLED IN MY GRISLY FIND via police radio enroute to the victim's home. It would be an item for the sheriffs, and I was glad for that. I didn't know how many more of these my department could handle without zonking out. Things were already bad enough.

Murray's widow was sprawled beside the pool in a teeny bikini when I got there, and she looked marvelous, which is an understatement. She was smooth as velvet all over, soft but not too, curvaceous but not exaggerated. It seemed even more certain, with the truth in full display, that she was too young a woman for Tim Murray.

I'd rung the doorbell several times and got no response, so I'd let myself in through the side gate, suspecting that I might find her back there. She rose to an elbow and twisted to one side at my approach, repositioned her legs and gave me a long, silent look.

"You're bringing bad news," she decided.

I hadn't thought it showed, but it probably did. I'd always hated a task like this one.

I pulled up a chair and sat down beside her, said, "Yes, I'm afraid so. Is anyone here with you?"

"My daughter is on her way over from Chaffey College, but don't keep me waiting. How bad is it?"

I took her hand and said, "Can't get any worse, Mrs. Murray."

"Please. Call me Patricia." She was cool as ice, which is often very misleading. "Tim always called me Pat and I never liked it. He knew I didn't like it, but he always called me Pat." I noted the past tense and wondered how long she'd been preparing herself for this moment. "Except when he was making love to me. Then he called me Patty, and he knew I hated that too. No, that's wrong, Tim never made love to me. Tim fucked me. He fucked me like I was a common whore. I never saw his penis soft. He always came in hard and ready, he fucked me in the dark, and then he left me. That is what life with Tim Murray has been. So don't take it easy with me, Mr. Copp. Exactly what has happened to him?"

"He was shot. Death was instant, I'm sure."

"I always took such good care of myself, exercised faithfully, played tennis and hated it twice a week, kept myself looking pretty for him. He liked to show me off, like one of his trophies. Do you know I haven't the faintest idea how much money we have? He never told me what his salary was. Gave me an allowance for the routine expenses, never quite enough to stretch from one payday to the next so I never had any just for myself. I was his housekeeper, Mr. Copp, and he condescended to fuck me once or twice a month when I behaved myself."

"Well, I—"

"I'm not shocking you, am I? That's okay, I shocked

myself awhile ago. Didn't realize I had sunk so low until I saw it in your eyes. I mean when I asked you about Lydia Whiteside. I don't know why I did that. It couldn't possibly matter. It has been one woman after another for the past twenty years, so how could it matter? But I always wondered . . . was he making love to any of them?—or did he treat them the same way he treated me? Was he shot in the head?"

"Yes."

"Odd how it comes out that way, isn't it? That was what he feared most. I don't think he was afraid of death. But he was afraid of being shot in the head. Was it in the front or the back?"

"Squarely between the eyes," I replied quietly.

"Uh huh." She lay there and stared at me through a moment of silence, then scrambled to her feet and said, "If you'll excuse me for a minute, Mr. Copp, I want to get into some clothes. If I suddenly shatter, I don't want to be dressed like this. Will you come inside with me?"

I went with her into the house and helped myself to a Coke from the refrigerator while she threw on a dress— probably right over the bikini because she was back before I got the can open. I've had considerable experience in this kind of situation—notifying the widows—but this one beat all. It had me off-balance, waiting for the emotions to break through that stiff layer of self-defense, wondering how the hell to respond to the embarrassing chatter.

She took a Coke, too, and sat on a stool at the counter, holding the icy can to her forehead.

I said, "If you've had any reason to suspect that Tim may have been in trouble . . ."

"Trouble?" she replied numbly. "Trouble—yes, he's been in terrible trouble his whole life. Trouble, you see, was Tim's middle name. If he didn't have trouble, he went out and found some. Do you know that I have been a single parent for nearly twenty years? I raised these children all by myself. I'm surprised that he could keep their names straight. Oh, let's see, Keith must be the boy—that's a boy's name, you see—and Kelly must be the girl. Well, isn't that neat! Mr. Copp?"

"Yes?"

"It hurt me terribly when I saw that look on your face."

"Which look was that?"

"When you learned that I had left here this morning and did not even know that my husband had not come home all night. That hurt, it really hurt."

"Sorry 'bout that," I said, with a forced smile.

"But this does not hurt. I can say that. It does not hurt. I don't know he's dead, you see, any more than I didn't know that he didn't come home last night. Tim did not really live here, you see. He merely slept here, now and then. So you can leave any time you're ready to leave. You don't have to stay here and hold my hand. I am not going to shatter."

"Feel like talking some more?"

"Okay. Sure." She popped the can and took a swig of the Coke. "Go ahead."

"How old are you, Patricia?"

"I'm thirty-eight. Got married at eighteen, straight out of high school. Had a baby at nineteen, another at twenty. What else do you want to know?"

"You're in great shape for thirty-eight."

"Well, it hasn't been easy. Tim likes them young. I believe he lost interest in me the day my pregnancy began showing. He was thirty when we met and I was sixteen. He likes them best at sixteen. Because at sixteen they're too *stupid* to realize how inadequate he is as a man, a real man. An artificial man likes them very young, you see."

"A girl down at the club awhile ago told me that your husband was always a perfect gentleman."

"Who told you that?"

"Didn't catch her name. She waits tables."

"That explains it. The whores always think he's a perfect gentleman. If I sound bitter, Mr. Copp, it is only because I am *very* embittered. Tim Murray was no gentleman. Never. Tim Murray was a selfish son of a bitch whose own comfort was always the first priority. He was playing handball with his cop pals when I delivered Kelly and he was in the mountains with his nursing pals when Keith was born. And *that* is the whole story of our lives."

I sighed and said, "Well, let's make it his epitaph. So ...what now for you? You know nothing about your financial position?"

"Well, I guess I do have some money, after all."

"You do?"

"Yes. It's out in the garage. Found it last week, I guess it's still there. In his locker. But what can I do with it? How do I explain where it came from?"

"How much money are we talking about?"

She waved a hand and said, "I don't know. Go look in the tan locker in the garage. The bottom lifts out from the inside. It's down there."

The garage was off the kitchen. The "locker" was a double-door metal cabinet of the type you see in business offices for storing stationery and the like. The "bottom," indeed, lifted out. The six or so inches of dead space was about four feet wide and maybe eighteen inches deep. It was filled with money, not new money, old bills which had seen many hands—fifties and hundreds in thousand-dollar packets.

Mrs. Murray had followed me and stood watching as I examined the cache. "How much would you say?" she inquired casually.

"Maybe a hundred thou," I told her.

I reinserted the bottom shelf and closed the doors on the cabinet. We returned to the kitchen. She sagged onto a stool and asked me, "Where does a policeman get that kind of money?"

"Only one place I can think of," I replied.

"It's why he was shot, isn't it?"

I said, "There's probably a connection."

"What should I do with it?"

"Let it sit for now," I suggested. "Let me try to find out what it means."

The daughter came in about then. Even if I had not been expecting her, I would have known who she was. Almost a carbon copy of the mother, adjusted for age. An absolute knockout. She looked at her mother, and at her mother's bare feet and slightly disheveled appearance, at me, and then said, "Oh, wow. Don't let him get away. I'm leaving."

Her mother said, "Don't be silly, Kelly. This is Chief Copp. He's filling in for your father at the department. He's brought us some bad news, I'm afraid."

The daughter gave me a stricken look and said, "Daddy's dead."

I said, "Yes."

She said, "Oh God, I knew it." Her eyes were wide, staring but seeing nothing. She dropped onto a chair and bent forward to massage an ankle. "Didn't I tell you?"

"Yes, you told me," Mrs. Murray replied in a mechanical voice.

"I get these dreams," the daughter explained to me. "I had another one this morning." A tear popped out of one eye and slid quickly along the smooth cheek. "We've known it was going to happen. We just didn't know when. And then I had the dream." She looked at her mother. "What time?"

The mother looked at me. I shrugged, said, "Probably early morning. I saw him about three o'clock. He was okay then. I'd say somewhere between three and eight."

The daughter said, with considerable animation, "Okay, I saw him at about five o'clock."

I said, "You saw him? Where?"

"In my dream. He was naked. When I see someone naked, they have just died. Wasn't it about five o'clock when I called you, Mama?"

"A few minutes past, yes."

"He was dead, then," the daughter said, and released another tear.

It was all too weird for me. I was gathering myself to leave when Mrs. Murray asked me, "Can he have a department burial?"

"I believe it would be appropriate," I replied. "I'll see if I can set it up."

"Don't mention the locker yet," she said, with a flick of the eyes toward the garage door. "Wait until he's buried."

I gave her an OK with the hand and let myself out.

I've seen a lot, and I've seen a lot of weird, but I'd never seen anything like those two.

Tears I can handle, screaming and anger and denial I can handle, but I didn't know what to call this.

Someone told me—oh, years ago, I don't even remember who said it—but I was told that you can know a man by the reactions of those who mourn his passing.

But I still did not know Tim Murray.

And I hoped I never would.

CHAPTER 14

I HAD A MECHANICAL LUNCH AT A DOWNTOWN COFFEE SHOP, don't even remember what I ate. I was a total stranger there and I was glad because the place was buzzing over the events of the night. Apparently the news of Tim Murray's murder had not yet hit the streets; I heard a couple of dark hints between tables to the effect that the ex-chief was still running the department and was probably "behind" the latest intrigues. It seemed that most of the patrons here were local business people who worked in the neighborhood—probably merchants, since it was a Saturday and also because the old downtown district had suffered the same fate as many other towns and cities in the age of the shopping malls. Nothing really exciting went down those streets anymore. There were a couple of small drugstores, a barber and a beautician, a shoe repair shop, two florists, a few small cafes and a saloon, several dress shops, a second-hand book store, other odds and ends of small, struggling businesses—all confined to a three-block area. The consensus of downtown—if that luncheon crowd were representative—was that Tim Murray was responsible for all the political unrest in the city.

I wasn't ready to buy that much, and I was not ready even to buy the ex-chief as a crooked cop, the money cache at home notwithstanding. Too much had happened too fast to take it all in with any sense of reality. I was not ready to seize any conclusions—especially not the way the downtown merchants were leaping at them. I'd spent the greater part of my life trying to fashion realistic theories from odds and ends of evidence, and I'd learned the hard way that "evidence" is not always as it seems to be. Ask a professional stage magician about that, if you doubt me.

The news wasn't in the streets but it had draped a black mood over the Brighton PD. You could feel it in the air there, almost an atmosphere of doom. People failed to meet my gaze as I walked through, what few were there, and I could even sense the mood in the usually alert dispatcher's office when I stopped off there to check the logs. No one spoke of it—and there did not seem to be much conversation about anything else, either.

Which was okay with me, I'd wanted time to brief myself somewhat before the scheduled one o'clock meeting with the narcotics squad. There were ten of them, down from a standing twelve as of the deaths of Hanson and Rodriguez, the two who'd gone after me. Sergeant Dale Boyd had been in charge since the reorganization three years earlier.

These guys did not answer police musters, didn't attend uniformed ceremonies, were rarely seen around the PD, and were virtually autonomous. That was not good, even I knew that—and I say "even I" because I had always chafed over the rigid layers in the normal police chain of command. Sometimes that can be frustrating to a hard-working cop trying to do his job with maximum efficiency. But no squad or detail or even division should be allowed to operate without a system of oversight in place.

The Brighton narcs had been doing a hell of a job, though. If the record meant anything, they were a highly skilled and smoothly efficient team, executing with great precision and almost remarkable results. The only disturbing element I saw in the record was a high incidence of fatalities among suspects during busts. These were covered, of course, by official shooting reviews conducted by the trio of captains, and every shooting by the narc squad had been found justifiable.

I might add here, however, that shooting reviews in many departments are regarded as mere technicalities to be observed for the record, in case of lawsuits by suspects or their families; in such departments, it is rare indeed to see an officer disciplined for unjustified use of his firearm, and it is not all that unusual for a department to routinely "clean up" the reports as a coverup of blatantly excessive force.

I felt that I was ready for the one o'clock meeting, but I doubt that I would ever be "ready" for Dale Boyd. He's about six feet tall, weighs close to three hundred pounds, I'd guess—but obviously hard all over, except maybe in the paunch—full red beard that points off the chin an inch or so, curly red hair to the shoulders, piercing blue eyes. A biker, a Hell's Angel, that's the image—all the way to combat boots, field pants, leather vest, chains, and earrings.

I did not see the eyes until I suggested that he remove his sunglasses—the reflecting type in which you see only yourself as you're trying to make eye-contact with the wearer—and then the effect was almost startling. I wondered idly if he wore colored contact lenses to produce that effect. I'd never seen eyes that blue.

The other guys you could see on any narc squad anywhere, the usual nondescript, scruffy bunch that has become so characteristic of the undercover cop wherever. You can't blame "Hill Street Blues" for that look; in that case, art indeed was imitating life. These guys are chameleons; you can't expect them to look like Wall Street bankers when they want to blend into the street environment. Behind the scruffy appearance, though, you find some damned effective cops. I knew that these guys met the criteria. They had me sized and slotted coming in, knowing me in a single look—and I knew that because I had their size too.

There was not room enough in the office to seat them all. No problem; some haunched down with their backs against the wall and one of them leaned against the door. Their leader was seated directly opposite me, at the desk. I introduced myself, didn't ask them to do the same, told them: "I've just been reviewing the stats." I looked directly at Boyd. "You guys have been doing a hell of a job."

He nodded and showed a smile, I think, and told me, "We reviewed yours too. Takes one to know one, doesn't it?"

I said, "I know a hell of a cop when I see one."

He said, "So do I."

"Two of your boys went down hard last night."

"Yes. It happens. We'd rather it went the other way but . . . when it comes, it comes."

"Those two tried to go the other way with me, Boyd."

"Yeah?"

"Yeah."

"Mistaken identity?"

"Oh, I think not. They tried. They missed. I think some-one didn't know they missed. I think someone had them set up in a stolen car. And I think someone put the car on the hot sheet and arranged the confrontation that resulted in their deaths."

"You've done a lot of thinking."

"It's the instinct for survival. Maybe all of you boys should start thinking that way."

"We're not boys."

"Boys to me," I told him, and allowed each of them to encounter my gaze. "*My* boys—for awhile, anyway. But I can't do all your thinking for you, not even for the short term. So I worry." My eyes clashed with the piercing blues. "Who've you been reporting to since Murray left?"

Boyd replied evenly, "I keep in touch with the watch commanders."

"Who've you been *reporting* to?"

"I file the reports through Marilyn DiAngelo. She was Murray's secretary. Yours now, I guess. Met her yet?"

"From now on," I told him, "you submit your opera-tions plans to Captain Williamson and you follow his di-rection."

He didn't blink. "Yes, sir."

"I'm going to be thinking for you boys for awhile, all I can."

"Thank you, Chief."

"Murray is dead."

That time, he blinked. "His heart?"

"No, I think it was his wallet. The sheriff will be looking into that. Feds too, probably, if they can get a toehold. How clean are you, Boyd?"

He blinked again. "I'm clean." The blue gaze flicked over his squad. "We're all clean."

"Let's hope so," I said. "The shit is going to be coming

down the pike, and it's going to find every sewer that isn't covered. You think about that. Each of you think about it. Okay, that's all I have."

Boyd held his seat, piercing me with quizzing eyes as the others stirred and left, then he got slowly to his feet and said in a low voice, "I don't know what Murray was into, but we're clean."

"He wasn't," I replied in a voice that matched.

He stared at me for a couple of ticks then turned away and went to the open doorway, turned back for another look and to mutter, "Thank you, Chief."

I couldn't tell if he was patronizing me or if he was genuinely reaching toward me.

I showed him a solemn wink as my reply, and he went on with that.

Very cagey guy.

I didn't know what the hell had been accomplished.

But at least I'd given those guys something to think about . . . and I believed that they were thinking.

I CALLED CAPTAIN RALSTON in and told him to postpone the firing review that I'd insisted be scheduled for that afternoon. He was not hostile but also he was no friendlier—maybe a bit sulky, though, as he replied, "I guess that would be advisable, under the circumstances."

I said, "That's what I thought." He nodded and took a step toward the door but I called him back and told him, "Patricia Murray requests a department burial. Since it's our department and the rest of the city is in disarray, I guess it's our decision. What do you think?"

"I guess it's up to you," Ralston replied in the same sulky voice.

"Get off it," I said harshly. "I need some input here.

How do your officers feel about Murray? Will they turn out for him?"

He shrugged and said, "If you tell 'em to, they'll turn out. I wouldn't feel too good about it."

"Why not?"

"I've never felt that Murray had the good of the department at heart."

I said, "That doesn't compute. I came in here last night and looked around and I said to myself, 'These guys have it good.' It shows, it's that obvious."

"Murray didn't do it," the captain insisted. "He never ran this department. Just threw money at it to make himself look good. I never thought he was much of a cop, let alone chief."

"Yeah, I heard that all before," I reminded him. "But maybe it's all sour grapes. Maybe you guys with the brass didn't like getting passed over. Maybe Murray was a solid guy with the troops."

He said it softly and with emphasis: "Bull *shit*."

I sighed and chewed the idea briefly. "Check with the coroner. I'm putting you in charge of the arrangements. Find out when they will release the body and send an undertaker to take charge. I want a hero's burial, honor guards and the works. Put the word out. Oh—and notify the neighboring departments, the sheriffs—Riverside, San Berdue, L.A.—let them know we'll expect a contingent from each."

"What the hell are you doing this for?" Ralston asked despairingly.

"Not for him," I said. "For her."

"Her?"

"The widow. She put in her twenty even if he didn't."

Ralston said, very subdued, "I guess she did."

I grabbed the telephone and turned him loose. He went

out while I was trying to find the number I wanted. The day was still young, and a lot needed doing.

I got her on the second ring, responding with a breathless, almost expectant urgency. "Yes?"

"This is Joe Copp."

"Who?"

"Lila's new chief. This is her sister, Cleo?"

"Yes. But I still haven't heard from her and I'm going crazy. They just announced on the radio that Chief Murray has been killed. Is that true?"

"It's true," I assured her. "It's very important that I find your sister. Help me find her."

She said, "I've called everywhere I can think of. My God, I . . ."

"Think again, then," I urged. "Forget the usual places. Try the unusual. Where would Lila go if she wanted to drop out for awhile?"

"God, I—is she in trouble?"

I said, "She could be. The last time I saw her she had just left a meeting with Murray. That was at about three o'clock this morning. I think Murray died shortly after that. Yes, she could be in trouble. And, dammit, just because she's a cop doesn't necessarily mean that she knows how to handle it. I've got to get to her. Let's say she felt she needed time to sort things out, without interference from anyone. Now, where does she go?"

"She might go to Arrowhead," the sister said immediately.

That would be Lake Arrowhead, an upscale mountain resort area north of San Bernardino. I asked, "Does she have a place there?" I was thinking cabin or condo. The high lake is less than an hour by car from Brighton. It is not unusual for folks of average means to invest in vacation property up there.

But the sister replied, "No, but she usually stays at the little inn right there in the village, the one just up from the traffic light. I don't remember the name..."

"I'll try that. Relax. It'll be okay. But if you think of anything else, let me hear."

"You'll be at the police station?"

"If I'm not," I said, "leave a message. Mark it urgent. But let's keep it cryptic. Don't give out info to anyone but me, not even to one of the cops."

She said, "I understand."

I wondered if she did.

I wondered also, idly, about the name "Cleo." Had to be short for Cleopatra with "Delilah" for a sister. Another interesting family, no doubt.

I wondered about that all the way to Arrowhead.

CHAPTER 15

I TOOK MY OWN CAR, an old Caddy, for the drive to Arrowhead. Didn't want to take an official car that far from its own turf. Besides, I prefer the Caddy to most newer cars. It's old but I keep it running and looking good, it's comfortable, and we fit each other. I recently modernized it, too, with a car phone. That is not a luxury these days, it's a necessity—especially in my line of work—and the cellular systems are really very good now.

The drive up into the mountains can be very pleasant if it's not during a peak season—which is summertime, with the schools out and families freed for camping and fishing vacations, and the winter holidays, ski season. During those periods the crowds and traffic can be even more hectic than down among the population centers. Spring and fall can be very nice, though, and in ten minutes flat you can leave the swirl behind and find yourself in almost isolated splendor.

This was September. The climb north up along the four-

lane state highway to the village of Crestline was quick
and easy, going from almost zero elevation to somewhere
around four thousand feet in about ten minutes. At this
point, you've already left the world of smog and grime
behind. From Crestline you swing back east and continue
the climb along a two-lane roller-coaster course called "the
Rim of the World Highway"—and the views are spectacular if you dare take your eyes off the twisting roadway
for a sneak peek every now and then.

From up there you can see it all. I suspect that you could
see the lights of San Diego on a good night. By the time
you get to Arrowhead, though, you are immersed in nature, engulfed in it, swallowed by it—literally. This is an
area of densely wooded and plunging canyons. All the
roads and trails are built along these narrow, twisting
gorges, and you literally cannot see the forest for the trees,
not until you hit the lakeshore itself. The lake, you see, is
set kerplop in the middle of that dense forest. The shoreline
runs for something like fourteen miles and it is all private
property. So far as I know, there is no public boating access
to the lake. A development company bought and developed the land way back around the turn of the century,
parceled it up and sold it off, and there's a lot of money
invested up there, especially in the lakeshore properties.

On my way up the mountain, I put some toll on the
car phone to talk to a friend in L.A., a guy who specializes
in electronic intelligence. He makes a good living sitting
at home with his computer and developing information
for others who lack his equipment and know-how.
Wouldn't call him a "hacker," exactly, because he's definitely a pro and claims that his services are entirely legal.
I wouldn't know about that, and actually I've never worried a lot about it. There's no real privacy left for anyone
in this world today, not really. Anybody can get your vital

116

statistics any time they want them, all with total legality—
and someone could right now be sitting in some cubbyhole
office on the opposite side of the country somewhere scrutinizing your banking records, your driving record, or any
other record that exists, and you'll never know them as
they know you.

So I don't worry that much about the privacy issue
because privacy is largely an illusion anyway. I don't go
out of my way to abuse the data pools, but I do use them
when I need them. Right now I needed them. And my
friend in L.A. knew how to get into them. I put him onto
Harold Schwartzman, told him what little I knew about
the guy, and asked him to get back to me with a profile
as quickly as possible.

It was about two o'clock when I pulled into the village
at Arrowhead. I hadn't been up there in years but it didn't
seem to have changed that much. Spotted Lila's jeep immediately, and I knew how lucky that was. If she'd rented
one of the hundreds of cabins or condos that are scattered
along those canyons, I could still be looking for her. The
village itself, though, is quite small and clustered quaintly
in one small section of the shore. The inn where she was
staying was located right on the main highway and in the
heart of the commercial area. Has an old European coun-
tryside look, very pretty in a rustic way, lobby and restaurant in the main building—which must be fifty or sixty
years old—cabins arranged in neat rows up the hillside.

I parked beside the jeep and went into the lobby, told
the pleasant man at the desk that I was meeting Miss Turner
there, asked him to ring her room. He started to comply
then stopped himself, said, "Isn't that the tall, pretty,
blonde woman?"

I verified that, understated as it was.

He told me, "She walked down to the lakefront.

About—oh, ten minutes ago. She took the lower road."
He pointed, and I understood. The main road veers off at
an intersection just below the inn, proceeds in two directions to skirt the shoreline, but that point also marks the
entrance to the main shopping areas, and there are two
ways also to go into there. The higher part is designed
primarily for the convenience of residents, has a big supermarket and other commercial services. The part nearest
the lake is devoted to the tourist trade, with restaurants
and shops enough to delight the browsers for at least a full
day.

I left my car at the inn and went browsing, too, with
something other than gift items in mind. Even in September there were plenty of people in town so I really did not
expect to find Lila among the shoppers, but I was too
restless to sit and wait for her—and, besides, the air up
there was crisp and invigorating, the sun warming rather
than oppressing, and it was a good day for a walk. Tried
to put myself into her probable frame of mind, kept to the
lakeshore walk, found her at the far end sipping wine from
a longstemmed glass on the veranda at Woody's Boathouse, one of the finer restaurants of the area. It overlooks
the lake, huge place—seats more than a hundred, probably—done up very cleverly in nautical motif. The veranda
is partially enclosed. I was on the boardwalk, looking in—
but I could have touched her—when she raised her eyes
from the wine and our gazes clashed.

"Well, God dammit," she said, with clear disgust.

I said, "Stay right there," and went on around to the
entrance.

She was still there when I reached her table, and she was
mad as hell.

I sat down beside her. A waiter came over immediately.

I ordered a Coke and looked over the menu while waiting for it. The waiter returned with the Coke. I asked, "What's good?"

He said, "You can't go wrong here. What do you feel like?"

"What did she feel like?" I asked, indicating Lila.

"This time of day, the house speciality," he replied. "Steak sandwich. Chef uses the choicest tri-tip, slices it wafer thin, then grills it and stacks it on a French roll."

"That's fine. Medium."

"Onions and peppers?"

"Did she?"

He grinned and jerked his head in a nod. All this time Lila is totally ignoring me. I said, "Do mine that way too, then."

When he left the table, I said to her, "Stop acting like a baby. I didn't come all the way up here to play games."

After a moment she replied, "Why *did* you come?"

"I came because we really need to talk, kid."

"Can't it wait 'til Monday? I have 'comp' time coming. I took it. I'm off duty 'til Monday."

"Has nothing to do with duty," I told her. "Has to do with staying alive. Are you up on the news?"

"What news?" she asked grouchily.

"Tim Murray was killed this morning."

It was like she didn't hear it for a moment. I was about to say it again when she replied, "How did he die?"

"The hard way. Bullet between the eyes. Found him stuffed into the trunk of his car at The Dee-light Zone. End of delight for him."

"When?"

"I discovered the body late this morning, nearly noon-time. He was stiff."

Lila hadn't looked at me since I joined her at the table. She turned to me now with eyes brooding and said, "*You* discovered the body?"

I nodded. "I was looking for him. He hadn't been home, so I went back to the joint. His car was still there. So was he."

She asked, "Have a suspect?"

"Not yet."

"Let me give you a clue."

"Okay."

"It started with Mayor Katz."

"What started?"

"The killing."

"Uh huh. And?"

"And that's your clue."

I said, "Katz was killed during a robbery."

She shrugged. "Maybe. Maybe not. Doesn't matter. It started then."

"And your pal Murray . . . ?"

She flicked me a disdainful look. "We weren't pals."

"No? Pardon the hell out of me but it looked that way last night. Why'd you go to Helltown?"

"I wanted to set up a meeting with the mystery man."

"Which mystery man is that?"

"Harold Schwartzman. Came to town three years ago. Dropped in from nowhere. Built that big place on the hill, started buying up other real estate. Bought into Helltown, big. Nobody really knows anything about him. He deals through intermediaries, holding companies, corporate covers. I believe he corrupted Mayor Katz."

"Why do you believe that?"

"Because that is when Brighton started going to hell. That's when all the fighting started. That is when Chief

Murray became an absentee chief. And that is when our department started falling apart."

"Could be coincidence," I suggested.

She gave me another of those looks. "Sure. And it could be coincidence when you see smoke and fire at the same time."

"So you've got a theory."

She sipped at her wine and spoke around the rim of the glass to reply, "Not much. Just started wondering about it all when . . ."

"When what?"

"When the chief got fired."

"And . . . ?"

"And nothing. Hey, I work vice—okay? I throw my hips on a streetcorner and invite the cruisers to proposition me. What the hell do I know about . . . ?"

I said, "No, I think you're more than that. Why'd you go running up to Schwartzman's mansion last night?"

The waiter brought our sandwiches, interrupting the conversation with an apologetic smile, inquired, "Can I get you anything else right now?"

I gave him a wink and a shake of the head, looked to Lila—she formed a "no" with her lips; the waiter gracefully withdrew.

But the flow was broken. Lila began munching on her sandwich and I didn't ask the question again right then.

It *was* a hell of a sandwich. It seduced me, showed me how little I'd eaten during the past twenty-four hours. So I ravished it with gusto, then washed it down with several cups of coffee. Lila had been watching me with some bemusement, maybe even amusement, our conversation limited to the merits of Woody's house special. It's not easy to eat a sandwich like that one daintily; she managed it, then remarked during my third coffee, "Some cops lose their appetite on murder cases. Yours doesn't seem to have suffered."

I told her, very soberly, "I've known some cops to even lose their sex drive."

She said, "You must have not known the same cops I've known."

"How does it affect yours?" I asked, still sober.

"I'm not going to answer that," she said. "You'll have to find that out for yourself."

I said, "Okay. When?"

She dabbed at her mouth with the napkin, opened her purse and checked her lipstick, said, "What's wrong with right now?"

"Your place or mine?"

"I don't know about your place but mine is a fantasy come true. It's nestled into the trees, it's *very* secluded, it comes with a hot tub built for two and a magnificent fireplace."

"Sounds like my kind of place," I told her. "Let's go check it out."

We did. But I did not forget for a minute why I had come up there. And, I suspect, neither did she.

CHAPTER 16

THERE IS SOMETHING ABOUT A PROXIMITY TO DEATH that sometimes heightens one's own sensual awareness of the joy of living. I'm no psychologist so I can't explain it, I just know that it's true because I have seen it over and over again and I have experienced it myself. You get that same effect from danger sometimes, too, like when you've just narrowly escaped death yourself, or during a crackling storm. Maybe it's fear-driven, I don't know, maybe it's just the reminder that life can be brief and its joys fleeting. But I think athletes experience it too, I know that cops do—routinely—and maybe that is why war and love so often go together.

Whatever, Lila and I had a hell of a go at each other at Arrowhead that afternoon. She attacked me with the same kind of hunger I'd shown the steak sandwich earlier, and God knows I love to be loved by a high-spirited woman. Surely her first orgasm was heard all the way down in the lobby of the main building, although the cabin was situated at least fifty yards up the hill. After that explosion, it was a continuing series of ecstatic waves in rhythmic sequence, punctuated by muffled yelps into my shoulder at periodic crests, then starting all over again without a pause—on and on into the sunset, until finally she gasped, "Please . . . Joe . . . that's enough for now. God, I . . . think I've broken something."

She hadn't, but I could understand how it could feel that way. I've always envied women their multiple orgasms. With guys, you know, twice is nice and three make you feel like Superman, but many women have a different mechanism. Get it wound up properly and it seems as though it could run on forever.

We had started in the hot tub and progressed to the bed, tried several different chairs and the couch, ended up on a thick, furry rug in front of the fireplace. Myself, I felt like I was broken all over and I'd even bled a little from teeth-marks in the shoulder. I guess we both briefly fell asleep in each other's arms on the floor because I did not remember it getting dark in there. The logs in the fireplace had been reduced to glowing coals, and that was all the light there was in the cabin when I came out of it. Lila stirred against me immediately and murmured, "You wanta try that one more time, Chief?"

I groaned in mock horror and suggested, "Check with my secretary. I might have a date open next month."

She laughed and snuggled, said, "I was kidding. I probably won't be *walking* 'til next month."

"That's what you get for fraternizing," I told her.

"Yeah. I changed my mind. Fraternizing can be nice." She giggled. "Am I still Lila Boobs?"

I sighed, told her, "That doesn't even begin to tell the tale. Let's see . . . what about Lila Rapture?"

She punched me in the ribs with a smooth knee and said, "Okay . . . Joe Cock."

I yelled, "Hey! Let's show a little respect for the brass here!"

I swatted her on the bottom and she jumped up squealing, ran to the bathroom. I drew myself together while she showered, put some more wood on the fire, pondered imponderable things while waiting my turn in the bathroom, then I showered while she picked the place up and returned everything to its rightful spot.

We toasted the rising moon from the window table and she hooked a foot onto my lap while we snacked on cheese and crackers from her duffel bag—then our eyes locked across the table, she smiled and I said okay, and we fell onto each other again. This time was slow, and gentle, and sensuous beyond belief. I held her in my arms and rocked her in a chair not made for rocking; she wept and laughed and cooed, and we became great friends. After that, we talked . . . and became better friends.

It was about nine o'clock when I kissed her goodbye, staggered through the dark to my car, and went back down the mountain. To those who may doubt the value of deep human communion, I can only say that you should try it before you knock it. And to those who would shame us for carrying on so, in the very shadow of death, I would like to say again that the very proximity to death can be a reminder that life is sweet only when we taste it fully.

I'd had a full taste, there on the mountain. I think Lila had too.

I WON'T SAY that I felt anything like Moses felt when he came down off Mount Sinai, but certainly I came down

125

from my mountain a lot smarter than when I'd gone up there. My talk with Lila Turner had been very enlightening, as much by its implications as by its content. And since it had been produced within that special golden torpor following fantastic sex, when two hearts are lying there beating as one, I had to give it at least ninety-nine percent credibility.

I'd asked her, "Why did you go to the mansion last night?"

And she'd replied, "Well, the first time I went because I'd been invited, and I was curious."

"What first time?"

"That was at eight o'clock. I'd heard about the parties up there but I'd never been to one. Then yesterday when—"

"Wait a minute. What kind of parties?"

"Just . . . parties, I guess. It seems that Schwartzman is one of these far-right-wing law and order men. Has a special feeling for cops. But, see, I think that corrupted some people. When a guy like that comes into a town like Brighton and starts flashing his mega-millions . . . well, it can be a corrupting influence, I think."

"Okay, so you were invited. Never before?"

"Never before, no. But yesterday—I was about to tell you—yesterday after that little charade with you at the supermarket, Peterson congratulated me on a job well done, and I guess he thought he was giving me a little reward. He handed me a—"

"Peterson's the one, the sergeant—"

"Investigations Unit, yes. He gave me a passkey and told me that the party started at eight. It was, uh, like I'd been offered some special privilege."

"So you went to the party. What was that like?"

"Well, I went because I think mainly I was just curious. I'd known about those parties—seems like every weekend they have a blowout up there and—well, to be honest, I felt good about finally being invited to one of them."

"So what was it like?"

"Just a bunch of cops sitting around the pool and drinking, telling tall stories."

"Was Schwartzman there?"

"No. He wasn't there. But Chief Murray was."

"Oh yeah?"

"Uh huh. And he came over and thanked me for setting you up for Peterson and Manning. Now this is going to sound crazy..."

"What?"

"It was like... he was still the chief. There were about twenty cops up there, and he was still the chief to all of them. You know what I mean?"

I knew what she meant, yes.

"It was like... he was still running the department. Through those guys."

"A leader in exile."

"Exactly! That's *exactly* the way it felt to me."

"Were the narcs there?"

"The narcs?" She wrinkled her nose. "I don't know. Not at the pool, I know, but... well, there were things going on inside too. So I don't know who all was there."

"Brass?"

"There was some brass, yes, couple of lieutenants for sure."

"You stayed at the pool the whole time?"

"Yes."

"Did you meet Lydia Whiteside?"

"The name is familiar, but..."

"Housekeeper, secretary, whatever. You know nothing about her?"

"Okay, yes, I've got her now. She used to—I think she

was a public steno or something like that, ran a telephone answering service—something like that."

"In Brighton."

"Yes. Then Schwartzman I guess made her an offer she couldn't refuse. I've seen her around. That's about it."

"You've never met Schwartzman."

"No."

"But obviously Tim Murray had."

"Oh, sure. And he went to work for him immediately after he lost his job with the city. He acted like he was right at home up there last night, that's for sure. I'd say he's spent a lot of time at that mansion."

"Okay . . . you went to the party at eight. Then what?"

"I left about ten. Went home and went to bed. Got a call to come meet the new chief. I'd been swimming, hair was a mess when I went to bed, decided when I got home I'd get up early and repair it then—couldn't do a God damn thing with it, Joe, when they called me to come meet you. That's why I was late."

"So you came to the meeting. It ended with a hit on Peterson and Murray. Why'd you go back to the mansion then?"

"I wanted to talk with Tim Murray. *Before* the word got out about the murders, if possible."

"You stopped at a doughnut shop on Foothill and talked to some patrolmen."

"Hey, you were right on me, huh? That's right. They patrol north of Foothill at that end. I spotted them, decided to ask if they'd seen Murray's car recently. They hadn't. I figured, okay, maybe he's still up there, so I went on up."

"Why?"

"Look, Joe, I didn't like the odor. I felt that maybe I'd

been dragged into something I wouldn't want any part of. I had to know what was going on."

"But Murray wasn't up there."

"No. But quite a few were. I still had the passkey. Works the gate, you know? Slip it into the box, the gate opens."

"But you parked outside."

"Not at first. I drove in. But this time the drive was lined with cars. I didn't like the looks of that, didn't want to get boxed in. So I backed down and parked outside, went up on foot."

"What about the dog?"

"I didn't see any dogs my first time up there. Saw the warning signs outside but no dogs inside. This time the whole house was lit up, top to bottom, and a bunch of guys were standing under the portico talking. They were cops, Joe. I don't think they knew about Manning and Peterson, if the conversations meant anything. They were just socializing, so . . ."

I said, "Most everyone had left the meeting when Manning and Peterson bought it. Maybe they didn't know. Who did you recognize?"

"I think they were mostly from the patrol division, the ones that were standing outside talking. I don't know a lot of these guys by name."

"You didn't go up and join them? Why not?"

"I don't know, it just seemed . . . weird."

"So what did you do?"

"I kept clear. I wasn't on the drive. I'd cut across the yard. I was standing just down below them, in the dark. I stood there for a few minutes trying to get a sense of what was going on. It really wasn't a party atmosphere this time. I mean, it was very sober and . . . strained. I overheard one of the guys saying that they all should go down to Dee-light and talk to Murray about this new development. He meant you. I assumed, then, that the chief was not at the mansion. I wanted to get to him before those guys did. I hadn't been seen yet, I thought, and I was leaving when the guy came up with the dog. He pulled a gun on me. I tried to show my badge, explain who I was. He wouldn't let me, made me hit the ground in a spread. I think he was going to cuff me, but the dog was acting up and he was having a hard time holding him. He warned me that the dog would chew my face off if I made a move, and then he sort of disappeared in the darkness. I thought he was tying the dog to the fence. I heard three shots, quick shots. I jumped up and got the hell out of there."

"You didn't see any more of the dog?"

"I didn't see the dog or the man again."

"You keep saying 'the man.' Didn't you recognize him?"

"No, I don't believe I'd ever seen him before. Of course it was dark down there by the gate. I didn't get a really good look at him. Those dogs scare the hell out of me, Joe. I don't like them even when they're on my side."

"You didn't know what the shooting was about?"

"Not until later. I didn't know what it was when I left there. I went on down to see Tim Murray. You know the rest."

I didn't know the rest, but I was too busy thinking about what I did know to even wonder about the rest, at the moment.

"You didn't fire your weapon while you were at the mansion?"

"No. I pulled it when I heard the shots, but I didn't see anything to shoot at. So I just got the hell out of there.

130

Believe me, though, I would have shot that dog if he'd come back."

"These were close shots."

"Oh, yes. Couldn't have been more than a few feet away."

"But you saw nothing."

"I saw nothing. Wondered, sure, I wondered. I know what you're thinking. I'm a cop. Why didn't I investigate? Well, the place was already filled with cops."

"That's why you didn't bother to call it in."

"That's one reason."

"What's another?"

"Well... maybe someone was just horsing around. You know cops when they're drinking and having fun. I didn't know, so..."

"Why did you tell me that you had fired those shots?"

"I didn't tell you that."

"You let me think it. Why?"

"I guess I just wanted to keep things tight for the moment."

"Because you thought that Murray was still running the department by remote control?"

"I thought it was very possible. It has been a very weird situation these past weeks. The captains have been working twelve-hour rotations, putting in a lot of hours. They've been the acting chiefs, Joe, unofficially of course. I don't believe anyone *wanted* an acting chief, not for real."

"What have they been covering, Lila?"

"God, I wish I knew."

"But you think that Schwartzman is the key?"

"Don't you?"

I had begun thinking that way, yeah.

And I had another key in mind, too. I asked Lila to show

me the passkey to the mansion. It's about the size of a credit card, hard plastic with tiny holes designed into it. I asked her, "Mind if I keep this for awhile?"

"Keep it forever," she replied breezily. "I'll certainly never use it again."

Maybe I would. And I could not get back down that mountain fast enough.

Maybe I did feel a bit like Moses, after all.

But only for a little while.

CHAPTER 17

I STOPPED OFF IN SAN BERNARDINO at the coroner's office, found two young women holding down the Saturday night fort in there. Both were pleasant and nice, seemed impressed by my ID, made me feel very welcome. One was a technician, gal named Sue, and the other was a records clerk. They gave me coffee and complete access to the files, dug things out for me, discussed things with me.

I looked over the reports on Saturday's Brighton-centered carnage and compared the official findings. Franklin Jones, the guy who'd been killed on the mansion grounds, had caught three explosive rounds in the chest and had died instantly.

Both Manning and Peterson, the cops who'd rousted me earlier that day before I was even on the case, had each died of a single gunshot wound to the head. Two thirty-eight slugs had been recovered during the autopsies, but apparently not from the same gun.

The narcotics officers, Hanson and Rodriguez, had died

from numerous gunshot wounds. Their corpses had yielded a number of thirty-eight slugs also, fired from at least three different guns, as well as shotgun pellets.

Tim Murray had been shot once in the head with a heavy, powerful weapon—probably .44 Magnum or .45 ACP, determined by measurement of the entry wound. The slug had passed on through the skull, exiting at the rear, and it had not been recovered.

Then I got to Mayor Harvey Katz, who had died six weeks earlier.

Odd.

Katz had been shot once in the back of the head and the slug had exited through an eye socket, also passing through the throat of the woman who had died with him in the bed of a cheap motel in Helltown. But the woman had been shot in the head, as well, and with the same weapon. Two .45 ACP slugs had been recovered, dug from the mattress upon which the victims had died.

Both Murray and Katz had died of contact wounds, and so had the woman who died with Katz, meaning that the muzzle of the weapon was placed against the head before the trigger was pulled. This is usually indicative of a cold, execution-style killing.

The two detectives Manning and Peterson got it a bit differently. In the technical reconstruction by the coroner's men, each man had been shot at close range but not by contact, each had been looking directly at his killer, and they had not been shot by the same weapon. One or more assailants had approached each side of the idling vehicle to fire through the open side windows from a distance of no more than eighteen inches. This had been determined by the positions of the bodies, the angle of entry of the bullets, the absence of damage to the car, and the characteristics of the recovered bullets.

I thanked the women for their help and went on to Brighton, reached the PD about ten-thirty. There was a morgue-like atmosphere there too, much too quiet for a Saturday night. Several patrolmen were writing reports, two detectives at a file cabinet looked up and nodded as I passed. One was Zarraza, the homicide dick who'd befriended me earlier. He dropped whatever was occupying him and hastened to catch up with me so I stopped and waited for him.

"You're working long hours," I observed.

"Well, we're a little short," he told me. "And I need the overtime so I don't mind."

"What're you working?"

"All of 'em. This very moment, I'm pulling the total history on Frank Jones. He's the dog expert, worked for us for awhile."

I said, "Yeah, I remember. While you're at it, do something else. See if you can determine how many Dobermans they have up at the mansion. I saw two. I think maybe there ought to be three, but that's just a hunch."

"I'll check it out, sure. I wanted to tell you about the ammo. The explosive rounds. There's an outfit called Whammo that has been sending around free samples to the police departments in the area. The use of these rounds is supposed to reduce the danger of ricochet and innocent victims. They're designed to disintegrate on contact."

I said, "Yeah, I've seen them."

"But that's not their real effect. There's a tiny delay built into the explosive mechanism, so that it explodes not immediately upon contact but upon penetration. It's like inserting a small bomb inside a body cavity then detonating it. This department nixed them."

"Yeah?"

"Yeah. Mostly for political reasons, I guess. I tried a

135

few on the pistol range a few months ago, firing into a block of paraffin. You wouldn't believe what one of those rounds does to a block of paraffin. Anyway, two hundred rounds of those little bombs were left here as samples three months ago. I thought you should know that. Fifty rounds were used for official testing. Nobody knows what became of the rest of them."

"Pull a survey," I suggested. "Try to account for them, officer by officer."

"We're doing that."

"Any word on Murray?"

He shook his head, grim-lipped. "County has the jurisdiction. We're supporting, of course."

"Get all the details you can from county. They handled the Katz killing too?"

"Yes. That's odd, I hadn't thought of it that way, Katz and Murray were killed within a block of each other."

"There are some interesting parallels," I told Zarraza. "You might check into that."

There was a new look in his eye as he strode away.

The watch captain must have heard us talking. He came to his doorway, leaned against the jamb with his hands in his pockets, said, "I was wondering if you had abandoned us."

It was Roger Williamson. He must have come on duty at eight o'clock, relieving Ralston. I remembered what Lila Turner had told me about the twelve-hour rotating shifts. McGuire had been on duty when I came aboard about twenty-four hours earlier and apparently he'd worked until eight A.M. when Ralston came on. Which meant that Williamson had just come off a twenty-four-hour stand-down, coming on at eight o'clock.

"Isn't this routine starting to wear on you?" I asked him.

"What routine?"

"The twelve-hour rotation routine."

He shrugged. "Someone has to do it."

"I'm doing it now," I reminded him.

"Sure, but for how long? We'll go back to the normal routine when the city council gives us a good reason for doing that."

"Suit yourself," I told him, and went on toward my office.

The captain called after me, "Boyd got in touch."

I turned back to say, "Okay."

"That won't change anything, you know. I still won't know what those fucking guys are doing until they've done it."

"So fry them," I called back.

"Oh, sure."

I went on into my office and straight to the message board. I had given my computer pal in L.A. a contact code: "Mr. Harper has the file." His name wasn't Harper but I did not want anyone reading over my shoulder, so I'd set it up that way.

The message was there, yes, poked into my personal little electronic file from the switchboard. There was another one, too, from Carl Garcia, as cryptic as the other. "Saw your notices. Regrets. A-OK here. Will call again at midnight. Don Carlo."

It was a pet name I had for the guy up in San Francisco. He was an alumnus of San Francisco State, their football team was called the Dons, he was a football freak like me and I used to kid him when things were not going well for the Dons.

Those were my only two messages, and I'd been gone for more than eight hours. But what the hell . . . this was all a charade anyway. Nobody thought of me as really being in charge—probably not even Carl Garcia. These

137

cops were all just going along with the gag, humoring me. I suddenly felt like an ass. Almost turned around and walked back out the door, but then I caught myself, sat myself down and gave myself a talking to.

Didn't matter what these guys thought. I was involved now, like it or not. I had to ride it through, see it to a proper conclusion. Then the fuckers could fire me as quickly as they wanted to. But not these cops . . . not *these* cops. Maybe I'd never been more than a sergeant but I'd sure as hell been more cop than any of these people here who had gone beyond that. It's not the rank that qualifies you, and the qualifications themselves may not mean a damned thing when it comes to getting a job done.

I sure as hell would not curtsy to a Roger Williamson.

I went back to his office with a snarl, told him, "Get your God damned feet off the desk, you asshole. Put them on the floor and let them move your fat ass outside and into the night."

His eyes bugged at me and the feet came down but not to take him anywhere. "Are you crazy?" he growled.

"Yeah, I'm crazy," I growled back. "Crazy enough to be involved in this mess. If this really was my department I'd have fired you when I walked in the door a minute ago. Where the hell have you been all day? Someone has killed your mayor, someone has killed your chief, someone has killed four of your detectives and a former officer. What the hell are you doing about it?"

His face had gone beet red but the voice was under control as he replied, "Well, Jesus, Joe, we're doing everything we can."

"No, hell no, you're not doing anything but sitting around and waiting for something to drop in your lap. Why the hell aren't you out there kicking butts up and down the street and *making* something happen? Dammit,

Roger, this isn't even my department but I can't bear to put my feet on the desk with all this shit going down around me. How can you?"

He stood up, stretched, sat back down, replied in a surly voice, "You're right. I guess we've all been shellshocked for the past month." He took his gun from a drawer of the desk, stood up and put it on. "I need to catch some air."

It hit me then. The guy was scared. He was scared out of his skull. I blocked the doorway as I told him, "We can fix this. Level with me. What the hell is going on around here?"

He said, "Please, Joe, stand aside."

I said, "Hell no, I won't stand aside until you talk to me. What's going on? Is it Schwartzman?"

He blinked and said, "Is it what?"

"Is it that God damned mansion up there?"

He said, "I . . . don't follow you."

"Sure you do! Who's running the death squad?"

Williamson sat back down, ran a hand through his hair, looked at the desk instead of me as he said, "You're crazy."

"I'm crazy." I laughed at that. "You're the guy that's scared out of his skull but I'm crazy."

"You're talking crazy, yes."

"Crazy is as crazy does," I told him. "Just watch my smoke."

I went back to my office. I heard footsteps along the corridor moments later and looked out my door in time to see Williamson standing at the door of the dispatch office. He said something to someone there then went on outside.

I scooped up my phone and asked the dispatcher, "Where's the captain headed?"

"He said he was getting some air."

"Right," I said, and hung it up.

I felt a bit smug about that.

But I'd hardly settled back into my chair when the smugness vanished. The floor beneath my feet rolled as though by earthquake and the walls vibrated to the ear-splitting roar of a huge explosion. I lurched to the door and saw people running. Someone fell through the front door of the building with his clothing flaming; a patrolman leapt onto the burning figure, trying to beat down the flames. Someone up there yelled, "Oh *shit!*"

I don't remember moving from my office to the front of the building, I just remember colliding with Detective Zarraza as he danced back inside with a stricken face.

"Captain Williamson," he croaked.

The smugness was gone, yeah.

So was Williamson. Someone had wired a bomb to the ignition of his official car, and he'd caught more air than he'd bargained for.

Another Brighton cop was dead, and a civilian employee who'd been standing thirty feet away from the doomed vehicle had been severely injured.

It was about time, yeah, to call out the national guard.

CHAPTER 18

I TOOK PERSONAL CHARGE OF THIS ONE and it took the rest of Saturday to clean it up. The word got around fast and the scene was choked with off-duty cops within minutes. It looked as though the entire fire department had responded, as well, so there was a lot of confusion and churning around. I declared the entire police department "on duty" in an effort to secure the scene and establish a workable perimeter, put all those guys to work and gave them something useful to do.

There was much to be done.

Adding to the confusion, I'd considered it wise to call in bomb squads from the county and from two neighboring cities. I wanted every official vehicle in the yard checked for explosives. Damned good thing, too, because they found another bomb. They found it in my car, my official car, which had been left behind in its reserved space when I took my personal car up the mountain. After that find, we sent the dogs throughout the building and into adjacent areas within the compound, also sniffed down city hall and all the vehicles parked over there. Found nothing else, but the sergeant in charge of the sheriff's bomb squad seemed very pleased with the one they did find. They were able to disarm it and take it to their lab for study. He told me, with a sober wink, "Someone's got a real hard-on for your department. This thing would blow up a tank."

They took it away with my blessing. It could represent valuable evidence and I wanted nobody but the best to mess with it.

Both Ralston and O'Brien were on the scene early and they'd been busy working with the evidence teams. The shattered body of Captain Williamson was transported to the morgue at about midnight, the shattered remnants of the car were hauled away, the visiting bomb squads departed, the fire department had withdrawn, and a crew of workers were neatly boarding up a number of the building's windows that had been broken by the explosion. There was not much more to be done, at the moment. I collared the two captains and we went in separate cars to a bar on Foothill for a drink and some quiet conversation.

The drinks notwithstanding, it was a sober group who huddled in a quiet booth at the rear of the bar at a few strokes past midnight on that Sunday morning.

Ralston muttered, "It's gone totally crazy."

O'Brien seemed to agree with that assessment. "Where's it going to end?"

I told them, "To get to that, we should decide first where it started."

"It started with you," Ralston glumly observed, meaning me.

"No. It started before me. I was called in here to stop something already started. What was that?"

Neither captain seemed to have a response to that so I suggested, "It started three years ago. It started with Harold Schwartzman. Would you agree?"

The two locked eyes with each other for a moment then Ralston said, "The man has been a disturbing influence, I'll say that, but I don't see..."

O'Brien added, "He started with Tim first. Then I think it spread to the mayor and some council members. But I never saw anything kinky. Okay, sure, you start flashing money and broads around a bunch like we have here, it can get a little out of hand sometimes. But Schwartzman had no reason that I could see to want to buy this department. The only local business interests he has are down in Helltown, and that's county jurisdiction, so..."

"Maybe he has political ambitions," I suggested.

"I've seen no evidence of it," O'Brien replied.

Ralston: "No, I think it's all been totally innocent. I think he just enjoys being a big fish in a small pond."

"Tell me about this guy," I requested.

"Schwartzman?" It was Ralston. "Not much to tell, other than... well, he cuts a low profile. Very important man—very busy—in and out of town a lot, I gather. He—" "Old or young?"

Ralston: "I couldn't say."

"You never met him?"

O'Brien: "I don't think I did."

Ralston: "Well, now wait a minute... I think once, maybe a couple of years ago..."

I said, "Get off it, you guys. You've both been up to that mansion probably fifty times. What is this? What are you covering?"

"I'm not covering anything," Ralston replied, miffed. "Schwartzman is not in town a lot."

"He throws parties *in absentia*?"

The guy glowered back at me. "That's right."

"You guys are nuts," I declared. "You get what you deserve."

I got up and walked out, totally disgusted with the both of them. They were covering something, for sure. Meanwhile their department was being decimated, and probably from within. Maybe they were next in line for a morgue tag on the toe, and they probably knew that too because both were shaken and obviously demoralized. But they were frozen in place. By something. What?

The answer came as simple and uncomplicated as most truths are, and it came from the blue.

They were frozen in place by their own personal involvement in whatever had been going down within that department.

And they did not know where to turn.

I WENT STRAIGHT to the mansion, got there at about a quarter to one. Lights were on inside, but just here and there, not like the night before when the whole place had been ablaze.

The key worked the gate, I drove in, parked beneath the portico. Lights were on out there but the grounds were in darkness. I unholstered my gun and stood with the car door open for a moment, wondering about the dogs. Heard nothing, saw nothing, no other cars were in evidence.

I briefly considered my options and decided on a soft entry, used my gadget to defeat the locks on the front door and let myself inside.

The entry foyer was softly lighted and I could hear the murmuring of a television somewhere to the rear, toward the kitchen area. I went back there to check that out, almost walked into the arms of a guy who was emerging from another small room back there. He wore a pistol in open leather about the waist, carried a flashlight, didn't look terribly surprised to see me. I asked him, "Where's Lydia?"

"Think she went to bed," he replied. "I was just coming to let you in. What's up?"

"We need to talk," I told him. "Let's go back inside."

He said, "Okay," and I followed him into the room. Maybe it had been originally designed as a pantry. Now it was obviously a security station. Three CCTV monitors were mounted into a console that covered a wall. There was room left for a swivel chair, a small table, and a filing cabinet. One of the monitors was displaying the gate approach, another was showing an automatic scan of the grounds in surrealistic infrared, the other covered the entrance to the house. I noted a stack of videocassettes on the table and a small portable TV off to one side. Some old movie was on. The guy turned off the portable and turned to me with an expectant look.

I had not seen this room during my first visit and none of the investigating cops had mentioned it to me.

"I'm Joe," I told the security guard.

He said, "Yeah, I think I saw you here before."

"Probably not," I said. "I've taken Tim Murray's place."

He said, as though he should have known, "Oh! Sorry. With all the excitement..."

"Yeah, we've had plenty of that," I agreed. "Who was in here last night when it went down?"

"Well that was Frank, Frank Jones. Or at least he had the watch. I guess he got called out. And that's when it happened."

Don Pendleton

I said, "Seems that way, doesn't it? How often do you
patrol outside?"

"Well, I just walk the wall maybe once or twice a shift,
or when I see something doesn't look right. We don't get
bothered much up here."

"You got bothered last night."

"Sure did. Glad it wasn't on my watch."

"What do you think happened?" I decided to cultivate
the guy. "As a pro, I mean, your professional opinion.
What really happened?"

"Well, I been looking at the tapes," he replied, almost
eagerly. "They don't show much. But I have my own idea
of what went down."

"That's what I'd like to hear, uh—what'd you say your
name is?"

"I'm Norm Tomkins." We shook hands. The guy
seemed very nervous. He pointed toward the stack of videocassettes. "Shows a loose dog. Frank really loved those
damned dogs. I think he took one out just to walk it, give
it some exercise, and I think it picked up something at the
wall. Now we're supposed to keep the dogs kenneled during onboard activities. They're really dangerous as hell,
you know. Me, I don't like them. I think that was all a
terrible mistake last night." He pointed to the tapes again.
"I see some guys running down the drive off the portico,
a couple more breaking across the lawn. This is before the
shots are recorded. I think those guys heard the dog raising
hell and I think they went to investigate. The shooting
itself doesn't show up on the tapes. But the sound of the
gun does, with all those guys running around in the dark.
I think that's what happened."

"What is what happened?"

"I think it was an accident."

146

"You think someone shot Frank, mistaking him as an intruder?"

"I think so, yeah. Friendly fire, as they say. Why else would he get shot?"

"What was the onboard activity last night, Norm?"

"Oh well, you know, it was the board meeting."

"Uh huh."

"Very important business."

"Uh huh."

"Those guys would be a little uptight. You know."

I said, "I know, yeah," but I didn't.

"I think someone just got trigger happy. Have they arrested anyone?"

"Nobody came forward, Norm," I told him with a cryptic smile.

He smiled back and said, "Yeah, I getcha."

"Guess I'd better take a look at those tapes."

"Well, suit yourself. But they don't show nothing." He went to the stack, scooped off the top three cassettes, handed them to me.

I said, "Thanks. Lydia went to bed, huh?"

"I think so."

"Anybody upstairs?"

"I don't think so."

"Maybe I'll go see."

He showed me a crafty smile. "If you find some, send some down for me."

I showed him a crafty smile in return, told him, "If you don't mind sloppy seconds."

He laughed, and I laughed, then I took my tapes and went upstairs.

CHAPTER 19

THE LIGHTS WERE ON IN SCHWARTZMAN'S MASTER SUITE and it looked pretty much as I'd noted earlier except that the litter had been cleaned from the top of the desk and the videocassettes had been removed, all of them. The cabinet was still there, beside the bed, but it now stood empty where earlier it must have held fifty or more of the hand-labeled cassettes. Bed looked a bit rumpled, as though someone had maybe sat on it, but the linens were still clean and crisp, unused.

A sliding mirrored door on the huge walk-in closet stood slightly open. I went in there and looked about, was impressed again by the number of suits hanging in rows like in a men's store, the shoes all in a row placed neatly beneath each suit. The image of that jarred something in the brain, made me take a closer look. Those shoes were not all the same size. Neither, I discovered a moment later, were the suits.

Well, well.

Wondered what it meant.

The suits, I supposed, could mean that Schwartzman had a weight problem—kept gaining and dieting, gaining and dieting. I knew what a problem that could be for a guy of average means. But if you're a millionaire . . .

That did not compute, though, because the size range was just too wide. You could not study the man's clothing and come up with a picture of him in the mind.

The shoes did not compute either. One's foot may swell a bit wider and fatter with obesity, but I could not understand changes in shoe size from a seven to a thirteen.

I filed all that away for later cogitation and went to the desk. It had three drawers on each side and a slim one in the middle. All were totally empty. There was not even a piece of lint in those drawers, not a pencil, not a scrap of note paper. The drawers even had that new wood smell to them.

I was getting disturbed.

There was no personal signature to this room. Not that it felt unoccupied, but that it had that air of occupancy you get from a hotel room. No photographs, no odds or ends of keys or coins, no individual imprint.

The bathroom was no better. But now, this was one hell of a bathroom; don't misunderstand. Had twin, built-in vanities, two private toilets plus a bidet, giant bathtub with a Jacuzzi and a double shower, a long ell with exercise mat and massage table. But it had that same impersonal stamp to it, not because there was nothing personal there but because too much personal was there.

Both vanities were stocked with masculine accessories, the usual stuff like shaving cream and aftershave lotion, deodorants and colognes, hairspray and toothpaste and all that stuff, even a couple of grooming kits for a mustache. But there were four different brands of shaving cream, three different aftershaves, maybe a dozen different deodorants and five or six colognes, four different brands of hairspray . . . you get the picture.

But there was no way to draw a picture of the occupant. So was that by design or . . . ?

It's no big deal, you might say—a guy with all those bucks probably doesn't do his own shopping anyway, maybe he isn't habituated to any one particular brand of aftershave, maybe he likes to smell differently every day, maybe . . .

Sure, you can run the list of maybes, and I did, but still I was left with a feeling of discomfort. I was going for a *sensing* of the guy, and you can usually get that from personal effects, from surroundings and decor, from the intimate items of bath and bedroom, if not anywhere else. Sometimes you can get it just from a car, from a profession, from a pattern of friends or colleagues. Most people put a stamp on who they are, and the stamp is made up of things they do or like or use or wear.

So maybe the stamp I was looking at had been built by a multi-faceted personality, and maybe that in itself was the stamp—but that did not account for the clothes closet.

The police mind often defeats itself by its own sensitivity. Sometimes we see patterns that exist only in our own minds, but it is our job to look for patterns because we are so often removed once or twice or thrice from the facts and events that produce or have been produced by the patterns we see—and sometimes those patterns are no more than phantom structures thrown up by the mind in a search for understanding.

So I was wondering, as I stood there in the center of that multi-personalized bedroom, if I was seeing a real pattern or merely creating one from my need to know. Either way it was bizarre, pal—really bizarre, and I did

151

not wish to give it much credulity at the moment, so I squelched it, thinking maybe I was reaching for straws, and turned the mind to other things.

I sat on the bed and called my computer pal in L.A. The hour never mattered to him, he always told me—call any time—but I woke him up and he sounded a bit surly at first.

Yes, he had the package on Schwartzman but he'd have to go downstairs to get it, so would I mind calling back at about eight o'clock, he'd just been having a terrific dream in which he was cracking the access codes to the Kremlin and he'd love to get right back to that.

"Can you do that?" I asked him.

"Do what?"

"Go back and resume a dream?"

He said, "Sure. Can't you?"

I said, "Well, I guess I never tried it."

"I do it all the time," he said. "Sometimes from one night to the next. It's just a matter of focus."

I said, "Sure. So how 'bout focusing on my package for a minute, first. You don't have to get up. Just give me the gist."

I heard the click of a cigarette lighter, knew that was what it was because this guy lives in a cloud of smoke. He coughed and said, "The gist is this. Many, many megabucks scattered around the world under many flags and too many corporate covers to penetrate in a casual sweep. I could do that if you wanted to give me a week. Knowing you, you can't afford it—so this is the budget tour, my friend. Panama, Nassau, Zurich, Frankfurt—and maybe that's just the tip of the iceberg—all coded accounts with only very wispy links, but take my budget gut hunch, they're all Schwartzman and they are all with no visible means of support."

"What do you mean, no visible—?"

"It's a laundry route, Joe."

I said, "Okay. What's the source?"

"Your guess is as good as mine but I think maybe Panama's the base."

"Drug money," I guessed.

"Well, there's a suggestion of arms too. The Frankfurt link. I think maybe Mideast connections but I haven't followed that."

I said, "This is getting wild."

"Well, you asked me for it."

"Yeah, but—I don't give a damn about—I've got a local problem here, pal. I'm thinking saloons and whore houses and porn shops, you're giving me international empires."

"Don't fault me, I started with your local problem. I only had what you gave me. He arrived in Brighton with a letter of credit good for two million dollars from this bank in Nassau. The rest fell out of that."

"Well, bring it back home for me."

"Can't do that. The man doesn't exist back home, only his influence. Doesn't have a social security account, no driver's license, no car registrations or loans or mortgages, no—"

"Hold it," I yelled, "You're making me dizzy. You're giving me the little man who isn't there."

"Exactly," he replied. "He's a fucking phantom, Joe. But he exists in the electronic networks. I suspect that he is not an American national."

"What would you guess, then?"

"I'd guess German, or maybe German by way of South or Central America. That's what I mean, though, when I say you can't afford it. It would take me a week to bust through all the protective layers. That house he built there in Brighton, for example..."

"Yeah?"

"Uh, yeah, the escrow shows . . . uh, I need to get the file."

I said, "Forget the damned file. Just give me the facts."

"The facts," he replied tiredly, "is that I need the file to read the facts. It's sort of squirrely. You know how these escrow things can get. Uh . . . he paid cash for the land and hired this outfit in Riverside to build the house . . . it's uh . . . I can't remember the name of the builder but you should be able to get that locally and it probably isn't important except that he bought the land as Harold Schwartzman and paid the builder as Brighton Holding, Inc. But now Brighton Holding, Inc. does not appear as a California corporation so I'd have to search other states to get that. Meanwhile there is an account right now in the Brighton City Bank under Brighton Holding and there is close to a million bucks in that account. I got uh, I got electronic transfers out but none in, and those transfers are all to Frankfurt, another corporation. It seems that the Brighton account is being fed from local sources and then siphoned off to Europe. So—"

"Where does Panama come into it?"

"Well, that comes from the original letter of credit from Nassau. The Nassau account is electronically fed from Panama."

I said, "Shit."

He said, "Yeah, it's a regular spiderweb. I gotta go back to sleep, Joe, I'm getting too far from the dream. Call me back about eight o'clock."

"Screw the dream," I told him. "I'm in a God damned nightmare here. Give me a quick profile on Schwartzman."

"I just did," he said, and hung up.

He just did, eh?

I sat there on Harold Schwartzman's bed and gazed

around Harold Schwartzman's bedroom, drew up a mental picture of his clothes closet and his bathroom—and I realized that, yeah, he just did.

He'd gotten about as close to the guy as I had.

Patterns?

Sure. A spiderweb is a pattern, isn't it?

A wardrobe of suits and shoes in eight sizes is a pattern, isn't it?

A supermarket of colognes and sprays and lotions overflowing two vanities is a pattern, isn't it?

I went back into the closet and yanked two suits off their hangers, smelled them, turned the coats inside out and smelled them again—picked up a shoe and smelled it too.

Shit. None of that stuff had been worn much, if ever. The coats did not smell of sweat or cleaning fluid; the leather of the shoes had never been wrinkled, the soles never soiled or scraped.

Then I looked at a label inside a coat. The label was from Paris. Another was from Buenos Aires. One from Rome.

Okay. Okay.

What was the pattern? Courier? Many identities, many personalities, many disguises?

Was that a pattern?

Did it fit anything in Brighton?

It did not, no, fit anything in Brighton that I could see.

But, hell . . . I hadn't seen anything yet.

155

CHAPTER 20

Lydia Whiteside's studio apartment was on the ground floor at the rear, near the kitchen but on the opposite side from the guard station. There was an entry there but also she had a private entrance from the outside and a small private yard/patio, and I later noted a parking pad for a car back there and a narrow drive leading to it off the main drive.

It was an ordinary studio apartment, nothing special, all contained within one room, alcove for the bed, small sitting area divided from the kitchen by a counter with two stools, small kitchen table for two by a window, whole thing furnished in Scandinavian Modern and ultra-personal in contrast to Schwartzman's suite—looked very much lived in.

In fact, the place was a mess.

Dirty dishes in the sink, clothing scattered around, at least a week's collection of newspapers stacked beside an easy chair, stacks of magazines and catalogs and opened mail filling the kitchen counter.

I found her in the alcove sprawled across the bed face down in a nightgown, one knee drawn up toward the chest as though she were about to crawl away.

But she wouldn't do that, couldn't do that.

She was cold to the touch and I could not detect a pulse. A powdery substance was spilled across the nightstand from a small plastic envelope, a little pile of pills beside an open bottle, an empty water glass—the picture was clear enough.

I went quickly to the guard station, told the guy in there to call the paramedics. "It's Lydia," I explained. "Tell them it looks like an O.D."

He cried, "Oh my God!" and dove for the telephone.

I went back and checked her more closely, satisfied myself that there was nothing to be done for the woman— she was gone—found what appeared to be a suicide note in a typewriter near the bed. A Colt .45 autoloading pistol was propped alongside the typewriter. I touched none of that stuff. The note wasn't signed and it had been typed on the back of a used envelope; read like this:

> *I killed Harve and Tim. No*
> *regrets. They were bastards.*

I growled out loud, "Sure you did," left everything undisturbed and returned to the guard station.

Almost collided with the guy again; we met in the doorway. He looked a little wild in the eyes, announced in a tremulous voice, "They're on the way. Is she okay?"

I sighed and said, "No, Norm, she'll never be okay again. When did you last see her?"

He backed into his room and fell into the chair, raised a hand to his face, chewed a knuckle for a moment—

collecting himself—finally replied, "I guess it was when the woman came."

"What woman?"

"I don't know what woman. Lydia told me she was expecting company, I should let her in when she rang."

"What time was that?"

"Must have been close to eleven. Because her friend was at the gate at eleven sharp, I noted it and logged it."

"Have her on tape?"

"Yeah, but it probably won't show much because I didn't see much myself on the monitor. She left her car down front with the headlights on high beam while she walked up to the gate and announced herself. All I saw was the glare of the lights, they faked out the camera and that's all I could see."

"Recognize the voice?"

"No, I don't think so. We could play the tape. I opened the gate and she walked back to her car and drove on in, went straight to Lydia's door, stayed for only about twenty minutes."

"What kind of car?"

"All I saw was the lights."

He was rewinding and cueing the video tape for me when the paramedics arrived. "You handle them," I told him. "I'll handle the tape."

So he went out to usher the medics through and I played with the video, found the spot, replayed the segment several times, had to agree with Norm. If it had been the intent to get through that gate without being recorded on video, it could not have been done any slicker. The camera was mounted in a housing and focused on the gate access. The brilliance of the car's headlights at high beam completely washed out the picture, and the car was through the gate and beyond the camera before the lens could readjust. As for the audio, it was clearly a female voice but muffled and virtually unidentifiable, uttering a single word: "Lydia."

A police unit came in almost on the bumper of the ambulance. I went out and talked to those guys for a minute, told them what I'd found and instructed them to secure the scene thoroughly, then I pulled Norm Tomkins aside and had another go at him.

"How well did you know Frank Jones?" I asked the guard.

"Not too well," he replied. "Just small talk now and then at shift change. We work funny shifts, to cover days off. Frank was really in charge. Of security, I mean. But he pulled rotations with us for time off. I didn't really know the guy."

"Like him?"

"Not especially."

"Is the pay good?"

"Oh yeah, no complaints about the pay."

"What do you complain about?"

"These nutty shifts. Plays hell with the social life. Sometimes we do twelve-hour rotations, sometimes twenty-four. 'Course, there's not much to do. I mean, we can catnap and that's okay."

"What about these dogs?"

He shook his head. "I don't want nothin' to do with 'em. Frank handled that."

"Frank handled it. What do you mean?"

"I mean the dogs were just for special things."

"What kind of special things?"

"Why're you asking me? Don't you know?"

I said, "What I know is what I know, Norm. Right now we're going for what Norm knows."

He replied, "Well, Norm knows nothing and you can count on that." He made a motion with the hand to simulate zipping his lip.

I gave him a knowing wink and went away from there. But I'll tell you straight from the shoulder, I did not know what the hell to make of any of it. And I was going just a bit numb between the ears. When you stop being shocked by the discovery of death, you know you're in trouble. And I had simply traveled beyond the power of shock. I was not really experiencing anything through the emotions—not sadness, not regret, not guilt or sorrow or fear or anything like that.

But I knew that I had to call Arrowhead and try to check on the movements of Delilah Turner.

So maybe I was experiencing a bit of fear, after all. I think, in fact, that I was scared numb over what I might discover about the tall, capable and beautiful policewoman.

HARVEY KATZ AND Tim Murray both had been killed by a shot to the head from a heavy pistol. A .45 Colt is a very heavy pistol. The thing that had stood out in my mind for some time already was the similarity in the way in which both men had met death. Both dead from a big bullet in the head, both wounds contact wounds. That would have been a stark similarity had the deaths not occurred six weeks apart and separated by the other killings. This way, it had come to mind more as an oddity.

Remember when I talked to Detective Zarraza about that? I was thinking execution-style deaths, and they did fit that pattern. But they fit another pattern, too, one in which the shooter is not that sure of his or her ability to handle a pistol properly. If you're not sure about that, the safest way is to place the muzzle right on the target before

161

you pull the trigger. That pattern would fit a woman such as Lydia Whiteside, assuming that she was not familiar with weapons, and apparently she had even produced the murder weapon and left it beside the confession, if you could call it that. Anyone could have put that scrap of paper into the typewriter and written the note.

I had to go along with the logic at least a little way and for a little while. It could figure that way. The murders of Katz and Murray did not have to be directly tied to the other deaths. They could be totally unrelated or loosely related without being tied. I had been going with a general assumption that the same person or persons were responsible for all of the killings from Katz on down. Now I had to consider the possibility that more than one game had been going down and that more than one solution had to be found.

Assuming, then, that Lydia indeed had killed Katz and Murray...why? Not simply because they were "bastards," though that could be a partial answer. When we kill, it is in anger, from fear, or for profit. Sometimes all three reasons coincide to produce a single murder, but for sure at least one of those elements is going to be present. I'm talking about sane people, of course, who otherwise observe the usual social norms and would not think of killing another unless provoked by irresistible forces.

Why would Lydia kill? More to the point, why would she kill the mayor and the ex-chief of police?

And if she had *not* killed them, why would someone wish to make it appear that she had? If there was a "death squad" in this town, which was already awash with human blood, why single out one or two of those deaths and try to shift the blame to someone else?

No, see?—the pattern was breaking, the connections

whipping in the breeze, the whole thing becoming more confused by the hour.

So maybe that, too, was a desired effect.

Of course, a painstaking investigation might reveal some very interesting interconnections between Lydia White-side, Harvey Katz, and Tim Murray—enough to provide all the answers needed to form a scenario for murder. Problem was, I did not have time for a painstaking investigation. My butt could be officially tossed out of town at any minute, and then God only knew how many more layers of concealment would be draped over the whole thing; the truth might never come out.

So what?—you might ask. It's no skin off for me. But that's where you'd be wrong. Someone had obviously tried to kill me, too, a couple of times—and there was no guarantee that they'd lose interest in me just because I'm tossed out of town. They would find the task much easier, too, once the local pressure was off.

So I had to ask myself the ultimate question.

Who wanted Joe Copp dead, and why?

"They" did. Because I'd been around too close and might have learned too much.

That simplified things.

All I had to do was find out who "they" are.

I guess that is why I felt so reluctant to call Arrowhead. There are times in a man's life, you know, when he'd really rather not know who "they" are.

CHAPTER 21

I MADE THE CALL FROM MY CAR and noted the time as one-thirty. It seemed incredible the things that had gone down in a mere twenty-four hours, but there it was. The voice at the inn's switchboard sounded sleepy but accommodating. I identified myself, then told him, "This is an official call. Do you understand?"

He replied, "Yes, sir, I understand. What can I do for you?"

"One of my officers, Detective Delilah Turner, checked into your place early this morning. Is she still registered?"

Without a pause, the clerk said, "She hasn't checked out. Just a moment, I'll ring—"

"No, don't ring her yet." I described her car, asked him, "Can you see it? It was right outside your window earlier today."

"No, sir, I don't see a car like that. I can step outside and . . ."

"Thanks, please do that."

The guy was gone for maybe twenty seconds, came back on to say, "There's nothing like that in the lower lot. There is other parking up above."

"Is your lower lot full?"

"No, sir. There's room down here."

I said, "I appreciate your help. Go ahead and try ringing the cabin."

I listened to about a dozen rings, broke in to tell the guy, "Okay, I'll catch her later. Thanks."

He wished me a good night and hung up.

I was having a lousy night, but that was okay. I'm accustomed to them. I went on down into town and circled the PD, saw no evidence of the jeep, decided—what the hell?—to take another fling at Helltown.

The jeep was there, yeah, where I'd hoped it would not be. I parked in a well-lit spot and ventured inside to almost the same scene I'd encountered the night before. She was even sitting in the same booth, this time with three guys whose faces I'd seen also the night before at my welcoming party. They were cops—patrolmen, if the memory was accurate—young, energetic, made me feel like Methuselah. There were beers on the table and the four of them were laughing and talking as though yesterday had never happened.

I dragged up a chair and joined them.

The merriment ended like a whimper and a cop on the outside gave me a guarded look as he greeted me. "Hello, Chief. You're keeping late hours."

I said, "Yeh. Goes with the territory, I guess." I looked directly at Detective Turner to add, "Don't let me spoil your fun." I looked around the crowded room. "Came to see Billy. He here tonight?"

Detective Turner showed me a puzzled smile as she informed me, "Yes, he's around."

"Been here long?" I asked her.

She shook her head. "Not quite a beer's worth."

One of the other cops signaled a waitress, pointed at me. She came over immediately. I told her, "I'll have what they're having."

"You'll be sorry," a cop said, grinning.

"That bad, eh?"

"Well, it's not that good, Chief."

"Why do you guys come here then?"

He shrugged, showed me a sheepish grin. "I like the girls."

I said, "Well, I guess that's better than liking the boys. But why does Detective Turner come here?"

She showed me a sober look, replied in a quiet voice. "She likes the boys."

It was clear that I'd spoiled their fun. Two of the guys stretched, said goodnight, got up and left. The waitress brought my beer. I handed her a five. She looked surprised, said, "Oh, no, it's on the house."

I put the five away, said, "What they like about this place is the price. Send Billy over, will you?"

The waitress smiled uncertainly and withdrew.

The other cop said, "Guess I'll be taking off too. Day watch tomorrow."

"Some guys have all the luck," I told him.

He said, "Yes, sir," and took off.

Which left me and Detective Turner. I moved on into the booth opposite her and asked, "Where the hell have you been? I've been trying to call you."

"Couldn't sleep," she replied, twisting her lips in a sour smile. "Is this an official interrogation or is it personal interest?"

"Call it personal interest."

"Then let me assure you that never have I been so loved,

167

so well, for so long. That said, it's none of your damned business where I have been since then." She was smiling when she said it but I doubted that she was smiling inside.

"Call it official interest, then," I growled.

"Same response," she said pertly.

I sighed, toyed with my beer, gave her a very direct look, asked her, "Have you been up to the mansion tonight?"

I saw something change in her eyes, something very subtle but also very telling. "Why?"

"Why? Because we have another death in the family, that's why. It's important. Were you up there?"

"No," she said quietly in a voice entirely devoid of emotion.

After a moment I asked her, "Don't you want to know who died?"

"I already heard about it. It's terrible. I heard there was a bomb on your car too."

"Oh, that one," I said.

"Terrible way to go. I guess. Do you suppose you feel it when you're being blown to pieces?"

I gave her another long, direct look. "That what you guys were laughing it up about when I came in here?— the look on Captain Williamson's face when the bomb exploded?"

She gave me a long one, finally said, "No, I think that had to do with the bomb in your car. What's going on here? Why are you looking at me that way? What are we supposed to do? We're all scared to death. What's wrong with that? And what's wrong with a few laughs to try to forget that we're scared to death?"

"You're right," I said.

"Thanks."

"Don't mention it."

I was rescued by Billy. He came over with a big smile, twirled the chair I'd vacated and sat down with his arms folded across the backrest, said, "Hi, Chief. I heard about Tim. That's terrible."

I said, "Yeah, there's been lots of terrible lately. Who did 'im, Billy?"

He hunched his shoulders and spread the hands in a mystified gesture. "If I knew, I'd tell you. That's straight and level. Let me tell you another. You earned my undying respect last night. I really like the way you handle yourself, and I don't just mean the fighting, I mean the class you showed afterward. So, anything you want . . ."

"I sort of want to stay alive, Billy."

He laughed, as though at a great joke. "Don't we all?"

"Did Tim send you out after me last night?"

"Yeah, Chief, he did."

"Why?"

"Didn't say why. Just said we should go out and take the son of a bitch down a couple of pegs." He laughed again. "Hell, we tried, didn't we?"

I said, "Yeah, it was a good try, Billy. No more than a couple of hours later, someone tried Tim and it was a much better try. Why, do you think?"

"Hell, I don't know. I just heard about it when I come to work today. I don't think I was here when it happened. When did it happen?"

"Somewhere around five o'clock."

"Well, okay, I was here I guess but Tim wasn't, I mean wasn't supposed to be. I didn't hear nothing, didn't see nothing. That what you wanted to see me about, Chief?"

"What time did you go home?"

"I went home at six."

"When was the last time you saw Tim?"

The big bouncer screwed his face into a thoughtful grimace, replied, "That would have been when he left, about four."

"He didn't leave at four. Time of death has been fixed at about five o'clock."

"Well, yeah, he left the club at four. I walked outside with him. It was four o'clock. I watched him drive away before I came back inside."

"He drove away? At four o'clock?"

"Yeh."

I said, "Billy . . . Tim was found dead in the trunk of his car. It was parked in his spot right outside here."

"When was that?"

"Late in the morning, nearly noon."

"Naw, I saw 'im drive away."

I said, "Thanks, Billy. Get lost, Billy. I need to talk to the lady."

He showed the two of us a big smile, said, " 'Til later," and left us to ourselves, left me also with something to think about, which is probably why I was not so quick and nimble in the conversation that followed.

"Boy, that's a switch," Lila said immediately. "Last time I saw you two together, he was about to take your head off."

"We came to an understanding," I explained. "Can't you and I do the same?"

She said, "I sort of thought we'd done that."

I said, "Yeah."

She giggled, covered her mouth with a hand, said, "*Oh, yeah.*"

"Lila?"

"Yes?"

"Why did you come back to town tonight?"

"That sounds like the title of a country song."

"Come on."

"I told you why. Couldn't sleep. And there is absolutely nothing to do in the mountains at night, this time of year. It's not that much of a drive. I'm going back up there tonight. I just . . ."

"Yeah?"

She sort of giggled again. "I came looking for you, Chief."

"And thought you might find me here at The Dee-light Zone."

"I tried the PD, you weren't there. Didn't know where else to try."

"Why were you looking for me, Lila?"

"Don't you know?"

"Well . . ."

"Sure you know. Haven't you been thinking about me too?"

I wasn't lying. "Oh yeah, quite a bit."

"What am I?—a nymphomaniac or something? Can't get you out of my head. Feel like I'm sixteen again."

I was feeling total despair. "Lila . . ."

"Oh boy, oh, there's that look, oh, wow—I've done it, haven't I. My *God,* how could I have said that!"

"No, it's not what you think," I said quickly. "Roger Williamson was not the last to die. I just came down from the mansion. Lydia Whiteside is dead."

She just stared at me.

"Did you hear me? Lydia—"

"I heard you," she said quietly. "So I guess I'm next."

"What does that mean?"

"I'm the next to die, Joe."

"Come on. What are you talking about?"

"Let's go back to Arrowhead. Right now! Spend the night with me."

I thought maybe she was kidding. "You die tomorrow?" I asked with what I hoped was a smile.

But she was entirely serious. "I die next."

"Over my dead body," I told her. "And that would not make you the next to die, would it?"

That thought seemed to give the brave, capable police-woman no comfort at all.

No, no comfort whatever.

And the Brighton patterns continued to fracture.

CHAPTER 22

LILA TURNER'S SURPRISING DECLARATION that she would be the "next to die" had come straight out of the blue, as far as I was concerned, and it had caught me a bit off balance. When I tried to press her for a rational explanation of the statement, she at first tried to laugh it off as a joke and when that did not work she clammed up entirely and refused to discuss it with me further. She was still obviously unnerved by the news of Lydia Whiteside's death, however, despite the earlier claim that she'd hardly known her, and a couple other minor points had been bothering me about the policewoman who had become my lover that very day.

The question of her midnight visit to the mansion twenty-four hours earlier was not totally settled in my mind. Supposedly she had gone there to find Tim Murray, had skulked around the shadows outside for a while, then left after first being accosted and detained momentarily by Frank Jones, who apparently had been shot and killed at about that same moment. In connection with that visit, she had lied to me at one point or another.

In Murray's presence, she told me that she had been the one who fired the shots that presumably killed Jones, but she'd created the impression that she had fired at the guard dog when it threatened her. Later, at Arrowhead, she denied firing any shots and told me that she had heard the shots nearby while lying on the ground waiting for Jones to tie the dog and take her in charge for trespassing.

I had doubted all along that Lila could have fired the shots that killed Jones because I had heard her car start just a couple of seconds after the gunfire. But the timing was off, also, to support her Arrowhead version that she was lying on the ground inside the gates when the shots were fired.

So . . . what the hell? . . . was Jones shot outside the gates and later carried inside to be found in a different location? Why? By whom? How?—I had buzzed past the drive myself hot on Lila's tail. I'd heard a ruckus inside as I passed, yes, but I'd noticed no activity outside those gates at that moment. Could he have been shot inside, from a shooter positioned outside, and then the body moved to a point where it could not have been *seen* from the outside? Again, why?

Or had Jones been shot earlier?

If so, where?—why?—by whom?—and why would Lila tell me that she had heard shots at the time to confirm the alleged time and place of death?

Had she gone to the mansion that night to see Tim Murray?—or had she gone up there to see Lydia Whiteside? And had she gone back again tonight, for the same reason?

Why would she tell me that she hardly knew Lydia, then

react so dramatically a few hours later upon hearing of Lydia's death? She'd handled all the other deaths okay, from what I'd seen.

And why was she stonewalling me now, when it must have been very apparent that I suspected her of lying to me? I walked her to her car, just as I'd done the night before, and I asked her, "Where did you go when you left here last night?"

"Home," she replied quietly.

"And?"

"And to bed."

"Uh huh. Then what?"

"You want me to account for myself?"

"I'd appreciate that, yes."

She said, "Go straight to hell. One afternoon of love does not get you that much."

"I'm not asking as your lover."

"As my boss? That doesn't get it either. If I'm a suspect then read me my rights and let me call a lawyer."

"You've been working with Tim Murray, haven't you? Since he was fired, I mean."

I might as well have been speaking to the wind. She went on to her car, inserted the key in the doorlock and opened the door, showed me a winsome smile. "Last invitation tonight. Come back to the inn with me."

I shook my head. "Can't do that, kid."

"Then I suppose this is goodbye."

"Don't you mean goodnight?"

She gave me a pitying look and got into her car, kicked the engine over. I walked alongside as she was backing out of the parking place—then decided, what the hell, to do something dramatic. I yanked the door open and dragged her out of the car. It coughed and died, which was more reaction than I got from her at that moment. I guess she was too surprised to resist or even complain. I kissed her and she stiffened at first, then relaxed into it and kissed me back. It got very passionate for a moment there, then I released her and I guess we were both a bit dizzy from the encounter.

"Does this mean you've changed your mind?" she asked huskily.

"Yes and no," I told her. I dug for my keys, took my housekey off the ring, handed it to her, gave her the address. "Can you remember that?"

"I guess I can," she replied. "What do I do with it?"

"Decorate it with your presence. I'll get there as soon as I can."

"This is your place?"

"Yes. It's about twenty minutes from here. Safer than Arrowhead, for the moment anyway. Be sure you're not tailed."

She said, "Joe . . . I can't do this."

"Why not?"

"Well, I just can't do it."

"I'll try to join you there in about an hour."

"Well, then, let's just stay together until . . ."

I said, "No, it's better that you go ahead."

"Promise you'll come?"

"As soon as I can."

"Promise you won't give me the third degree."

I held up my hand in a scout's oath. She smiled and got back in her car, blew a kiss as she drove away.

I didn't know if I was glad or sad.

I only knew that I could not turn her loose into the night again completely on her own. And I did not want her at my side when I returned to Lydia Whiteside's apartment. Another pattern was forming in my subconscious and I wanted to give it room to develop fully before trying to fit it into the world outside.

I STOPPED BY the PD and got an update on the Whiteside investigation. The homicide boys were still up there but the body had been transported and marked for autopsy. Zarraza was in charge of the investigation, which told me something right there. He was one of the low men on the totem pole, therefore this particular investigation was not being given much priority. But, of course, these cops were almost totally consumed by the deaths within their own ranks. Practically the entire operations division was mobilized toward those other investigations, and all of the detectives were putting in some wearying hours beyond and above the usual pace of work.

O'Brien had the watch. He seemed friendly enough, even when I told him that I was calling a halt to the unofficial "acting chief" rotation.

"Makes sense," he agreed. "Especially now with Roger permanently out of the rotation. And I have to tell you, I'm getting dog tired."

"Go home," I ordered. "Right now. Take the rest of Sunday off. I'll pass the word to Ralston and I'll want you both in here at eight o'clock Monday morning. Let's get things back to normal."

He said, "Well, that will take some doing, but I guess I'm ready to try."

"Then consider yourself on-call 'til Monday. Get some rest. Be ready to tackle a total reorganization when you come back in here. I'll expect you and Ralston to set it up. Let your lieutenants carry the load. I want you two on standard day shift and I want an equal distribution of responsibilities."

"Okay," O'Brien tiredly agreed.

"Who's your best man on the floor right now?"

"That would be Ramirez, but he's already been on duty around the clock. He's beat too."

I checked the time and told O'Brien, "Let's send most of these people home. You and Ramirez put your heads together and decide who completes the watch. Resume with the normal day shift, Sunday routine. Soon as you get that set up, send Ramirez in and you take off, go to bed, get some rest. You can put it all back together Monday."

"What if you're not here Monday?"

I showed him a smile. "What difference would that make?"

He smiled back. "See what you mean. Okay. Thanks." He took a step away, paused, turned back to say, "If I pegged you wrong, Joe..."

I grinned and told him, "No, I think you've had it right. I wouldn't like me either, Pappy."

"Asshole," he said with a smile, then went on to turn the watch over to the homicide lieutenant.

I spent the next ten minutes scrutinizing the logs and reading reports, then I went on into my office. Ramirez caught up with me there as I was collecting my messages, said, "Okay, it's set. Pappy said you wanted to see me."

I had him confirm that Ralston had been notified of the change, then I told him, "I want Zarraza for a special detail. Tonight. Can you cut him loose?"

He nodded. "He's working Whiteside. Just finished the on-scene. He's on his way in. What's up?"

"Can you find a judge in this area on a Saturday night?"

"We have a routine, yes. You want a warrant tonight?"

I said, "Search warrant. The Schwartzman place. Not

just the Whiteside apartment. The whole place."

"Oh, you want...?"

"Right, all grounds and structures, the whole schmear. Two deaths up there in two nights, you have all the justification you need." I glanced at my watch. "I'll need it by four o'clock."

The guy seemed just a bit disturbed about that. I told him, "If it's bothering you, spit it out. What's the problem?"

He came in and closed the door, leaned against it to tell me, "There's been a longstanding hands-off policy where Mr. Schwartzman is concerned. I don't know how high that goes, so...the apartment, okay—the grounds, okay—but Mr. Schwartzman's personal...I don't know that I can make a case for a search of all structures."

"You mean you're afraid you can't sell it to a judge."

"That's about what I mean, yes."

I said, "No judge in his right mind would openly obstruct a murder investigation, whatever his politics. Do it this way. We suspect that Franklin Jones may have been murdered in Schwartzman's home while he was away, or by a guest or intruder in Schwartzman's home during the commission of another crime. We absolutely must have a warrant to search the premises from top to bottom, and we must have it immediately to secure whatever evidence may be developed from the premises. Got that?"

"Got it," he assured me, but he still looked troubled when he left me.

I felt a bit troubled, myself, when I collected the electronic message that had been awaiting my attention since midnight. It was from "Don Carlo," it was short, it was cryptic, and it was disturbing as hell. Not because of what it said but because of what it implied.

The guy had sworn me in just a little more than twenty-four hours earlier, after all but imploring me to take the job. Now it seemed that he was firing me:

"The Dons lost again. Kill all bets, cut your losses. Better luck next time. Medicare isn't half bad. Don Carlo."

Not only that, but it sounded like maybe he was firing himself.

If I was reading it right, then for sure I would be running the streets naked and alone come Monday morning.

At least, now, I knew how much time I had to walk out of this town under my own steam, clean, and proud.

I had a little more than twenty-four hours. If I should live so long.

CHAPTER 23

It was getting onto three a.m. when Zarraza rapped on my open door and stepped inside. He looked tired, in fact he looked beat, and I could sympathize. He gave me a quick rundown on the results of the Whiteside investigation to that moment, which added nothing to my own understanding, and concluded by stating that the coroner's team was leaning toward a finding of death by self-administered drug overdose, pending autopsy results.

The security guard, Norm Tomkins, had given Zarraza essentially the same story he'd given me regarding the eleven p.m. visitor. Zarraza had the tape in an evidence bag but had not yet viewed it. I told him what I had seen on the tape, then handed over the three other tapes Tomkins had given me before the discovery of Lydia's death. I explained that they were the surveillance tapes from the period surrounding the shooting of Frank Jones, and I further told the detective, "Let's keep those under wraps for the time being. There are other tapes I'd like to get my hands on, but I want it legal beyond any question." I explained that I had sent Ramirez for a search warrant and told him, "I want a clean sweep, I want a fully preserved chain of evidence, and I want to make the move before Schwartzman returns. Also I'd like for you to handle it. Are you game?"

Zarraza smiled tiredly as he replied, "Well, at least the spirit is willing."

"Then the flesh will follow," I assured him. "Pick a couple of guys who you'd trust with your wife and your life. Have them ready to move within the hour."

He glanced at his watch, said, "None I'd trust with my wife, but I get your meaning. I know a couple I'd trust with my life."

I warned him, "If we find what I'm hoping to find, it could bring a lot of discomfort to a lot of people in this department. I'm not sure about Ramirez, even. Be sure you're sure about the two you pick. They should be squeaky clean and not afraid to see the chips fall where they may."

"Why're you so sure of me?" Zarraza asked with a faint smile.

"I'm not," I replied, mirroring his smile. "I'm following the gut. What else can I do?"

"That's what I'm doing," he said.

"Trust it?"

The smile broadened. "What else can I do?"

So at least we understood each other. "Put your men on alert, get them on board as quickly as possible. I'll tell Ramirez that the search warrant is yours. You move as soon as it is in your hands. I want all the tapes, surveillance and otherwise, and I want them cleanly identified as to where they were found and the condition in which they were found. I want all clothing, all papers and records and writings, anything and everything that can identify or verify the residents and/or visitors. You know what I want."

He knew, yes. "We'll need a truck."

"Cut a voucher and rent one, have it ready to roll by four o'clock. Will that be a problem?"

"No, I know where I can get one on short notice. Will you be coming up with us?"

"I'll be there waiting for you," I assured him. "How's the gut now?"

I already knew, seeing it reflected in his eyes. "Tumbling a bit," he admitted. "You're taking on big game, you know."

"Get the right weapon," I reminded him, "the rhino falls as quickly as the deer."

He knew that, too, and he knew that we were going for the right weapon.

I just hoped I'd picked the right team. Zarraza had called it. I was going for damned big game.

I WAS AT the mansion by three-thirty, passed myself through the gate and allowed Tomkins to open the front door for me. He was clearly frazzled, confused, frightened—and his frame of mind pre-empted my own agenda of the moment. "I think I'd like to get out of here," he told me as soon as I stepped inside the house. "But I don't know what to do. I'm supposed to go off at eight. Who's going to relieve me? I called Harry Snow and he says he's not coming in this morning. So who the hell is going to relieve me?"

I said, "Look at it this way, you'll get all this overtime. Is Harry sick?"

"No, he's scared, says he don't want no more to do with it. I even have to feed the damned dogs. The gardener's gone, the maids are gone—nobody will be back until Monday. What the hell am I supposed to do?"

"Who pays your salary?"

"Lydia took care of that. She managed the place. So who's running it now? Are you? Can you find someone to relieve me?"

"Can't you get hold of Schwartzman?"

He gave me an "are you kidding" look. "How would I do that? Are you in charge here now?"

What the hell—why not? I squeezed his shoulder reassuringly and said, "What do you think, Norm?"

"Well, I think someone has to be in charge. You said you took Tim's place, so . . ."

"And what did Tim do?"

"Well, you know . . . he ran it."

"The security?"

"Well, sure, that too. I just want to be sure I get relieved. Harry has freaked out and he's not coming back, I can tell you that, he's not coming back. I've been on ever since Frank died and maybe I ought to be freaking too. What's going on around here, Joe? Why would Lydia do that? Why would she want to kill Tim? Those two were as close as any two people you'd ever want to see. Why would she do that?"

I said, "Well, Norm . . . he *was* a married man."

"He was?"

"You didn't know that?"

"I don't know, I just assumed . . . when did he get married?"

I said, "We're talking about Tim Murray, right?"

"Right, Tim Murray."

"The Chief of Police."

"Right, that Tim Murray. But I didn't know he was married."

I said, "Maybe he didn't either, Norm. Maybe that was the problem."

"I wonder if Lydia knew."

"If she didn't know, maybe she found out the hard way. Maybe that was Murray's wife that came here just before Lydia died."

This guy was not what you'd call bright, but he wasn't that dumb. "Aw, no, I don't think so, Lydia really wanted to see this woman. Well, it's a hell of a note. It's got me very worried, Joe. I'd like to get out of here."

"I don't see any chains on you," I told him.

"Well, I can't just leave..."

"Why not?"

"Who'll feed the dogs?"

"Don't worry it. If you want to go..."

He did, he really did. "I'll lock the gates open. That okay? So the maids and gardener can get back in?"

I shrugged and said, "It's fine with me, Norm."

It was like the guy had just been granted a parole from prison. I saw the weight of unexpected responsibilities slip from his shoulders as he hurried back to his little cell. I stood at the front door and waited while he gathered his things, and I saw him out the door a happy man.

But probably only for a little while.

I'd brought a patrol unit with me. They were waiting outside to collect him. Another unit was already collecting Harry Snow, the other guard. For nothing, maybe, but at least they'd get booked on suspicion of littering or whatever and we could hold them for awhile, pending other developments.

For awhile, at least, Copp was in charge of the mansion.

*   *   *

FROM LYDIA'S APARTMENT, which apparently also doubled as a makeshift office, we took six boxes of records, receipts, account books, bank statements and other papers. Apparently she had been running two bank accounts with the local bank, one under Brighton Holding, Inc. and the other a personal account in her own name but nothing under Schwartzman. There were payroll records not only for the help at the mansion but also for a number of businesses in Helltown, including The Dee-light Zone, as well as account books and other records having to do with the management of those businesses.

I didn't take time to go through all that stuff. We just bundled it and bagged it and boxed it, carried it to the truck, and moved on to the rest of the house. I went through the maids' rooms while Zarraza and his crew cleaned out the security station, tried to not really disturb the meager belongings there and didn't expect to find anything but felt that I had to give it at least a tweak, then was glad that I did because I found something interesting if not exactly evidential. One of the maids had a photo on her dressing table, it was taken out about the grounds somewhere, and it showed an aged Asian man—probably the gardener—and a young Asian woman posing self-consciously with the swimming pool in the background.

In that sunlit background a man and woman sat at a table beside the pool. The man, I'm sure, was Tim Murray. The woman, it seemed, could be Lila Turner. Both wore swim suits, and the woman appeared to be caressing the man's shoulder.

I wanted to take that photo but I suppressed the urge, leaving it undisturbed in its small plastic frame; it was, after all, the private property of one who evidently possessed little else—but I went out of there with the photo etched indelibly into my gray matter.

The guard station yielded three years' worth of logs showing cryptic notations chronicling the comings and goings at the mansion—nothing at first look to get excited about—and surveillance tapes covering only about the past week. Apparently the tapes were "rolled over" on a weekly basis and used again.

Upstairs, though, Zarraza discovered a veritable bonanza of video tapes along with cameras and lights, the works. They had been stored in a locked walk-in closet especially outfitted for such storage, the walls lined from floor to ceiling with stacked four-drawer "video library" boxes, each carefully labeled as to date and time and subject. The cameras were state-of-the-art camcorders, looked very expensive, and there were eight of them.

Coincidentally, maybe, there were eight bedroom suites in the mansion.

"Look at the labels on here!" Zarraza crowed. "Do you recognize some of these names?"

Yes, I recognized some of those names.

"If this is what I think it is," he said, "these guys have to be out of their skulls, unless they never knew that they were on candid camera. This guy Schwartzman must be a total pervert! Look at all these tapes! There must be hundreds!"

His two assistants wanted to come in and take a look, and the three of them had a hooting good time as they scanned labels on the boxes.

I could not quite get up to their point of elation over the find, maybe because it was pretty much what I'd expected to find and maybe because I could not get the photo from the maid's room out of my head.

I told Zarraza, "Take your time with this stuff. Log it in very carefully. Do the same with the clothing and any other items you think worthwhile. Then I want you to take it all to San Bernardino and very carefully log it in there with the sheriff. Check each item into each evidence locker, be sure it's properly sealed."

Zarraza understood where I was coming from, and he was in total agreement that the evidence should not be stored in Brighton. But he said, with a glum look on his face, "It will probably take all day."

I knew that, and I also knew that I did not have the whole day to spend on it.

So I left them there at five o'clock on Sunday morning, to complete the task on their own, and I turned my sights toward home.

It was time for a showdown with Lila Rapture. But I decided on a small sidetrip along the way. It came to me that I needed, first, to have a little talk with a local politician.

CHAPTER 24

DURING MY EARLIER QUESTIONING OF NORM TOMKINS, the security guard, he had mentioned "on-board activities" and implied that special security measures were in effect at such times. He had also told me that the late Friday night gathering was a "board meeting," but the guy was talking cutesy with me, with a lot of insider smirking and sniggling, and I'd just let the remark pass over my head as talk to impress me by. I was being a bit "cute" myself at the moment, of course, and had not wanted to appear overly dumb or curious so I hadn't pursued the matter.

But now I was really beginning to wonder about the activities at the Schwartzman mansion, trying to form a coherent pattern in the mind which would explain what had gone so wrong with the city of Brighton. It seemed rather clear that the major troubles had begun developing at roughly the same time, three years earlier. At that time, the city had terminated its participation in the joint-agency task force for drug enforcement and initiated its own beefed-up approach to the problem, presumably after the mayor had become miffed over the division of spoils.

Coincidentally, Harold Schwartzman appeared on the scene with two million dollars in a letter of credit from a Bahamian bank, bought the land and built the mansion, cozied up with the cops and opened his mansion to them for parties and whatever even when he was not present to participate. He bought into Helltown, apparently employed a lot of moonlighting cops to help him run the businesses, and began funneling money from those businesses into an overseas banking network.

But Schwartzman himself was a wraith, a phantom figure who conducted all of his business under a variety of corporate covers. I could not even get a physical description of the man, and his Brighton home was more like a clubhouse for cops, it had no imprint which would reveal the personality or habits of the owner.

Apparently Tim Murray had been on the payroll even while still Chief of Police, perhaps as Schwartzman's "man on the scene" at Brighton—and maybe this was the first fatal mistake. Maybe he became less and less a cop, more and more a stooge for Schwartzman and an illicit international empire, and maybe he began seeing his own department as little more than a private force to protect his other interests.

It is very difficult to corrupt an entire police department, even from the top down. I had never known of one. But you don't have to corrupt the entire force if it is an efficient machine to begin with. You just need the key people, and that does not necessarily mean the brass. If you have the keys to the machine, you can run it in the direction that serves you best, and it will serve you while also serving the primary interests in ways that do not affect you.

So who were the keys at Brighton?

Depending on the nature of your own private operation, you might want a vice key, you might want a narcotics key, you would probably want a rather hefty patrol key and a very delicate investigations key. Of course if your interest is in stolen goods, you'd want a burglary key; if fraud and swindles, a bunco key. And, just to keep things tight and secure all the way to the top, you'd want a damned strong brass key.

So . . . if my pattern was forming according to the observed logic, I had most of the players pegged, most posthumously. Roger Williamson had been the brass key. Manning and Peterson carried the investigations and burglary keys. With Helltown so prominent in the background, I figured a need for a vice key and maybe even a narcotics key—so maybe Turner, Hanson, and Rodriguez would fit those locks.

Strange, isn't it, how patterns can form from seemingly nowhere? Ever watch clouds appear in a cloudless sky, lightning streak from cloud to cloud, raindrops appear like magic, streams and puddles form on dry ground, raging torrents inundate the flashflood areas and suck down victims to a watery death? An hour ago the sky was clear. But an invisible pattern was there nonetheless, and maybe even the victim's name was written in the empty space that quickly became the storm.

Maybe I had the wrong pattern in mind . . . but certainly I had the victims, I could see them as the effect of the pattern, and I was merely trying to reason backward to a probable cause—because I was not there when the clouds began to form.

If my theory was right, then the clouds probably began to form when a "reform slate" disrupted the cozy politics of a small town turned big, the mayor was very nearly unseated and two of his cronies were turned out of office.

That could put a strain on things, especially if the mayor and his boyhood friend whom he'd installed as the chief of police had sold their city to a highrolling international financier who was now using it in virtual asylum as the seat of an illegal empire.

In my reading at the time, I put Schwartzman's influence on the scene ahead of the decision to withdraw from the multi-agency task force. Brighton withdrew because they wanted to be able to call their own shots to the maximum possible extent, and it could be very difficult to "key" such an operation. So Katz and Murray prepared the ground and Schwartzman waltzed in. It would have been incredibly easy. And things probably moved along smoothly until the political clouds formed. Now all are vulnerable, nerves get touchy, anxieties arise . . . and thieves fall out.

The inevitable storm either produced or was produced by the death of Mayor Katz. The rest all fell like dominoes. Maybe not all in a direct line, there could have been isolated branch lines, but surely all began to topple when Katz fell.

And the panic within the total structure of corruption must have been great. *Panic* bugged the office of the new city administrator and learned that he was trying to contact a private eye named Joe Copp; *panic* moved to discourage the potential interloper from entering the private preserve; and *panic* then began disposing of the weaker keys when it became apparent that the interloper was now in charge and capable of bringing the whole house down.

Manning, Peterson and Turner were now the most vulnerable because they'd become exposed—so down went Manning and Peterson. But why not Turner?

I had assumed that the two narcs, Hanson and Rodriguez, had been hit in the mistaken belief that they had succeeded in hitting me; I now began to revise that scenario, and it seemed more likely that they were hit *because* their hit had failed and someone with a command key knew it, feared that I had recognized them, and got to them before I could get to them. A patrol key took care of that little necessity.

Why dissolve the brass key, Roger Williamson?

The captain was crumbling, and that must have been more evident to others than to me. The death of Murray might have hastened that process—but Murray was not a key, Murray had been the keeper of the keys, so why had he gone down? A branch line? Maybe.

Why had Turner not gone down? Because she was more nimble than the others?—faster on her feet?

A problem here.

If Murray indeed had been "in charge," as my logic pattern demanded, who was keeping the game alive now that Murray was dead? Had he ordered the bombs for my car and Williamson's car before he fell himself? Or was there a damage control group at work now, hoping to cut the losses and come out clean?

If Katz represented a branch line and Murray another, and both had died for reasons outside the scenario—if indeed Lydia Whiteside had killed them both for reasons of her own—wasn't it ironic that the entire chain of dominoes had begun toppling from a branch line?

But still there was Turner.

And why had she said "I'm next to die" when told of Lydia's death?

I guess I wasn't buying the murders of Katz and Murray as branch line events... which means also that I was not buying Lydia Whiteside as their killer.

If not Lydia, then who?

Was there really a "board" which had met in secrecy at the Schwartzman mansion at about the time that the latest round of killing had begun?

193

If so, of whom was it composed, what was its purpose, and who was its chairman?

Where did all this leave the nimble Turner?

And when the pattern finally resolved, where would it leave the romantically smitten Copp?

HIS NAME WAS Charles Calhoun, man of about fifty-five with very intelligent eyes and impressive bearing—even in pajamas and robe—and he was one of the newer members of the Brighton City Council. It was Calhoun's son, Richard, who had been arrested at the high school some ten months earlier on a charge of dealing drugs to the other students. The charges had been dismissed because of what the judge in the case termed "tainted evidence." Going purely on what Murray had revealed to me about the case, Calhoun had then embarked on a "vendetta" against the most visible cop in Brighton, the chief of police.

I realized that I was perhaps exposing myself prematurely to a potential enemy, but I rang Calhoun's doorbell at shortly past five o'clock on that Sunday morning, identified myself, and had a go at a better understanding of the city's problems.

It was easier than I had expected. The councilman graciously invited me in although a total stranger had just pulled him out of bed. We went back to the kitchen. He made coffee and listened attentively while I explained my presence in his city.

I told him, "Carl Garcia and I go back a long way. He called me Friday and told me that he was fearful of his family's safety, seemed to believe that his police force was infested with renegades, asked me to come in and take charge of the department subject to later approval by the council."

"I see."

"Uh huh. But I'll give it to you up front, neither of us expected me to win approval and I would not accept the job on a permanent basis for any price. I came because of Carl and I'll be out of here before the council can even begin to think about the appointment. I came to smoke out the renegades and—"

"With spectacular success, I'd say. I've known about you, Copp."

"Since when?"

"Since the hell began. I have a man in place over there, myself."

"Over there where?"

"At the PD."

I said, "Really. Who is that?"

"Never mind who it is, he's there and he's been keeping me informed. I'm a bit disappointed Garcia would believe he could smuggle a new chief in behind the council's backs. But I do understand the urgency and I'm willing to give some latitude here if it doesn't get too wild."

"How wild can it get?" I asked him. "We've had eight deaths in roughly twenty-four hours. If it gets much wilder than that—"

"No, I was referring to the degree of latitude as to the way you operate. My informant tells me that you are something of a maverick, that you cut corners and perhaps play a bit loose with the letter of the law but never with its spirit, and that you usually produce dramatic results. Don't get me wrong, I am not in favor of flouting legal procedure as an expedient to the processes of justice, but I see this as a war, here in Brighton, not a criminal justice problem, and one must make allowances in war."

I had allowed an amused smile to cross my face as he was speaking. He'd noted it, and I knew that he had, so I had to spill it. "The only guy I've known to speak like that straight out of a warm bed on a cold morning is a lawyer friend of mine. I was thinking about that. No disrespect intended."

"None taken," he replied, with a smile of his own. "Is my profession that obvious?"

I was warming to the guy. A bit stiff, perhaps a bit old-school, but at the same time warm and likable. "I would call it either lawyer or professor."

"So you're batting a thousand. I have been both."

"Now you're a politician."

"Every citizen is a politician," he lectured me. "Politics is no more and no less than the art of social intercourse. Law is its language."

"What is crime, then?"

"Crime is anarchy, chaos, the anti-society. That is what we have had here in Brighton in recent years."

I said, "Some may feel that crime is a necessity. A starving man will steal bread, no matter how much he may respect the law."

"It is still anarchy," the councilman insisted. "There is a social solution to starvation."

"What if no one gives a damn about the other man's hunger?"

"Ah, but that is crime too. Subtle, but crime."

I was not merely playing with the guy or indulging in idle debate; I was going for his size, and liking what I found. "Was Tim Murray an anarchist?"

He gave me a long, sober look, then took cups from the cupboard and poured the coffee. He motioned me to a chair, took one for himself, and said, "Yes."

"Mayor Katz?"

"Yes."

"Harold Schwartzman?"

"To answer that, we must first produce the *persona* for identification."

"Suppose," I said, toying with my coffee, "that the persona is nowhere in evidence. What if Harold Schwartzman is no more than the convenient concoction of a criminal conspiracy?"

He showed me surprised eyes, replied, "You've tumbled to that already?"

"I've considered the possibility."

"So have I," he said soberly, thoughtfully. "But do you want to hear something strange? If that is true, and I believe that it very well could be true, then I also believe that it might have begun as a completely legitimate police operation."

"A sting?"

"A sting, yes, that got out of hand. It seduced them, worked too well, they couldn't resist it. And when they got in too deep, it swallowed them."

"Have you seen anything to suggest that this could be true? I mean, other than sheer intuition?"

He nodded, sipped his coffee, replied, "I know that several million dollars of the police budget were approved and earmarked for expanded anti-narcotics operations a few years ago, and that there was no accountability for the use of those funds until the new council demanded it."

"So how was the money spent?"

The councilman smiled. "It was not spent, if you can believe a hastily produced record. The funds were 'on hold' in the Brighton City Bank, in a special sub-account. Guess who owned the account."

It did not require much of a guess. "Brighton Holding, Inc."

He smiled again. "There you go. So what would a policeman call it? Intuition? Or evidence?"

197

"What was the earmark?"

"The earmark was 'Drug War Covert Operations.' The money was not from the general treasury but from drug-bust confiscations. The stated intent was that the allocation be used to fund anti-drug sting operations. I believe that the money may have been used inappropriately, that it may have been used to seed other operations that were never recorded—operations which over the years may have yielded sufficient illegal profits to restore the initial allocation when it became necessary to do so."

I said, "And you believe that Katz was aware of all this."

"I have wondered," he replied thoughtfully, "if the entire council may have known about it. The old council, that is. The two who survived last year's election have been acting absolutely paranoid since their beloved leader, Harvey Katz, abandoned them in death. We are now in total chaos."

"I'm surprised," I said, "that you have not asked the sheriff or the attorney general to investigate."

"We've tried that, and I've been called everything from a Nazi to a communist and a pervert every time the question has arisen in council. These other agencies will not step in unless they are officially invited. Needless to say, no such invitation shall be forthcoming so long as the old guard can hold sway."

"So how did you get Murray out?"

"That came as quite a surprise. John Lofton proposed the removal. John was one of Katz's longtime cronies. I don't know why he turned on Murray. Certainly he has not switched sides on any other issues."

"Why didn't I come to you twenty-four hours ago?" I mused.

"Because I could not have told you all of that twenty-four hours ago," the councilman replied. "The pattern was much too abstract at that time."

"Say that again?"

"The pattern was—"

"Okay, I just wanted to be sure you said that. I've been flailing away at patterns ever since I came to town. Been wondering if I've been tilting at shadows. Tell me something. Why did you run for city council?"

He shrugged. "I live here. I'm raising children here. Someone had to turn the rascals out."

I reminded him, "You almost paid too high a price for civic pride. Why did Murray go after your boy?"

"He wanted me under his thumb. The arresting officers planted that evidence. Murray hinted as much when he came to me and baldly suggested that I and my family would enjoy the quality of life in Brighton much more if we were all friends and could depend upon one another in bad times. It was blatantly obvious that he was offering me a deal."

I chuckled.

Calhoun asked me, "What?"

I said, "They rousted a councilman."

"They tried."

"No," I said, "they did. And it turned around and bit them. These guys were jerks, Charlie."

His eyebrows raised a bit, perhaps at the familiarity, but he responded in kind. "Very dangerous jerks, Joe. Be very careful. It must be evident to you by now that they will stop at nothing."

I shrugged and said, "Well, I believe maybe they have already defanged themselves. Unless . . ."

"Unless what?"

"Unless," I said, "Murray lost control of his own operation a long time ago."

"If he did, what would that suggest to you?"

I sighed. "The king is dead, long live the king."

"And in his place . . . ?"

"A parliament," I said. "Or a board of directors. Without the savvy of the founding father, without the intelligent cautious restraints."

The councilman seemed to be enjoying the exchange. "What are you getting at?"

"What would you call it," I asked, "when the inmates take over the asylum, or when the cons take over the prison?"

"Naked anarchy unleashed?"

"Must be something like that." I finished my coffee, decided it was time to be on my way. "I think maybe it's also something like a pirate mutiny at sea. The crew takes over and the captain walks the plank. What are they now?"

"They're the bloodthirstiest bastards afloat," said the councilman-lawyer-professor.

"I think you're right," I agreed.

I thought so, yeah. And maybe that was what we had at Brighton.

Maybe the machine had become "keyed" for killing, and nothing would stop it now short of its own total destruction.

CHAPTER 25

I BOUGHT MY PLACE WHILE I WAS ON THE PUBLIC PAYROLL with the L.A. County Sheriff's Department, shortly after my third divorce and before the price of mountainside property began to inflate so ridiculously. I could not even begin to scrape up a down payment on the place the way the market is now and I'm probably the poorest guy in my particular neighborhood. I probably couldn't meet the payments that some of these other people are making on lesser properties. I have been told that I could cash out with an impressive windfall, and I've thought about doing that a couple of times—but what the hell, it's all I've got left that tells me who I am when I'm not at work.

With marriage, you know, I figure three strikes and you're out of the game for good. I am, anyway. Maybe I fall in love easily, and I can't recall ever falling out until I got kicked out, but it takes more than love alone to make a marriage.

They were all good women and I loved each of them

like crazy all the time we were married, but I guess I wasn't so good to them or for them. I'm usually a guy with sharp focus, my whole life has been that way, and I tend to get blind to anything outside that focus. With the kind of work I do . . . well, I've gone days and even weeks away from home and unaware of anything outside the focus of the moment. A woman deserves better than that, has a right to demand more than that. Marriage just is not workable with me.

My home, though . . . well, my home is very forgiving. It's gadgeted-up to run itself when I'm not there, the indoor plants are all automatically watered, a guy comes once a week to mow the lawn and keep the outside tidy. Meanwhile my imprint is there. I can be gone all week and when I get home I know where I am and who I am, and I feel welcome there.

I'm positioned far enough up the mountain that I can look down onto most of the whole Los Angeles basin, from the ocean to the deserts, and it is quite a sight when the atmosphere cooperates. I live at the dead end of a narrow, tree-lined lane, and I have acreage enough to run a couple of horses. I don't keep horses and wouldn't even if I had time for them, but I do like having the space and the closest thing to seclusion you're likely to find, these days, this close to the urban sprawl. I have neighbors but I'd seldom know it. We all respect one another's privacy and keep pretty much to ourselves, and that works well for me.

I opened an office down in the valley when I first went private, but then I've always had this informal office in my bedroom too, and it got to the point where I was taking more calls at home than at work. The outside office began to seem like an unnecessary expense—and now and then I'd have trouble coming up with the rent—so I closed the valley office awhile back and do all my business at home now. I like it better this way.

I remodeled the place myself, shortly after I bought it, as a bachelor home with a single large bedroom—it takes the same space as three rooms originally took—and I guess I indulged my innate hedonism when I built that room, put in a spa and a small workout area, other comforts. The outer walls are one-way glass, positioned to afford the spectacular views mentioned earlier. It can be very inspiring, and I guess it just naturally follows that I spend most of my time at home back there.

It was no surprise, either, to find Lila Turner dozing on the small sofa I have back there. It was six o'clock, the dawn had dissolved the night sky, and my sleepy-eyed visitor was a bit upset with me.

"You stood me up," she complained grumpily.

"No I didn't," I protested. "Here I am."

"Ta da, ta da, sound the trumpets, *he* has arrived. You sent me over here just to stash me. I resent that, Joe. I can take care of myself, thank you."

"Can you feed yourself?"

"No, and I'm starved. Think you could feed me?"

Sure I could, and I did. I whipped up some eggs in the kitchen while she freshened up in the bathroom. She presented herself draped in a towel from the armpits to the knees, helped with the bacon and toast, and we were devouring breakfast ten minutes after I'd walked into the house. Didn't talk much as we ate but there was a lot of eye contact and warm smiles. Obviously, she'd dumped her grouchy mood in the shower. She told me, as she mopped her plate with a scrap of toast, "I turned on the Jacuzzi."

I nodded and said, "Glad you thought of that."

"It will relax you. You look awful."

"Feel awful," I admitted. "But the food helps."

She leaned over and brushed her lips against mine. "There," she said huskily.

"There?"

"Yes. We kissed and made up. Doesn't that feel even better?"

I lied, of course, and said that it did when it really did not. It would take more than a meeting of lips to satisfy my mind about Lila Turner.

She said, "I love your place. Have you always lived here alone?"

"Uh huh."

"It seems so ridiculous... I don't know a thing about you. You could have been married, for all I knew. Joe, this is crazy. We are total strangers."

"Not anymore. I thought we covered the introductions very well up at Arrowhead."

"Our genitalia met. Big deal."

I said, "It was more than that, Lila. Wasn't it?"

She gazed at me for a long moment before replying. "Was it? I really don't know. Aside from Mighty Joe Copp, who are you? What do you like? What are your politics? Do you go to church? Which one? What makes you cry?— or do you? What do you read? Who do you admire? This house bowled me over, Joe. I don't know what to make of you."

I asked, "Did you think I lived in a dog house?"

She said, "Well, no, but I sure didn't expect to find the country gentleman."

"You didn't," I assured her. "I don't spend a lot of time here, Lila. This is sanctuary, it's refuge."

"From what?"

I shrugged. "You tell me."

She said, "You're a big phoney."

"Maybe."

"Sure you are. You come off as this big rough and tough cop with a badge for a heart, and all the time you're—you're..."

"What?"

"Well I don't know what. But I want to find out. Can we start all over?"

"Start what all over?"

"You know what."

I said, "Well, if you'd like to join me in the spa..."

"No, hell no!" she cried. "We don't need to start that part over!"

I tried to smile as I reminded her, "I sort of got the idea that part was what it was all about. Isn't that what you came here for?"

She said, "Maybe it was—okay, yes it was. But that is not what I am talking about now. I am talking about..."

"It's nothing to apologize for."

"Who said I was apologizing? Geez! Why are you making this so hard for me? You know what I'm trying to say."

I refreshed my coffee, tasted it, looked into those hot eyes, told her, "I usually don't have a lot of time for romantic protocols, Lila. So I sort of take it where I find it, when I find it. Yesterday I found something very special, and I'll always think of you the way I found you yesterday. Beyond that..."

There was a very long silence, during which Lila helped herself to more coffee and drank half of it before she said to me in a very soft voice, "Thank you for being honest about that."

I'd had some time to think about what I'd said, myself, so I told her, "No—bullshit, Lila—I wasn't being honest. It's partly true, that's the way it has been for a long time, but I really don't feel that way about you. You want me to be totally honest? Okay. Here's total honesty. I'm half-crazy with the way I feel about you. At the same time I'm half-crazy with the job I've taken on here. I am trying to isolate some really rotten cops and kick their asses behind bars where they belong. I don't know where you stand in that lineup, kid. You've been stonewalling and gaming me from the very beginning, you're still doing it, and I'm scared half to death that I'll have to kick your ass in the bargain."

"Would you do that?" she asked softly.

"If the ass is rotten," I assured her, "it will get a kick, not a kiss. Yeah. I'd do that."

"And what if it's not rotten?"

"Then I'd kiss it, and gladly."

She stood up, dropped her towel, turned her back to me and bent over in presentation. "It's not rotten, Joe."

I didn't kiss it, not then, but I chuckled and slapped it lightly, we both laughed, then I picked her up and carried her to the spa. We got to know each other, the right way this time, and then we talked of many interesting things—after which, yes, I kissed Lila's ass.

"WHEN DID YOU begin your investigation of Tim Murray?"

"The day after Mayor Katz was killed. I had this wild idea that Murray was behind it, that the investigation had been fixed, and I just couldn't stand it. So my investigation of Murray started as an investigation of the mayor's death."

"Who handled the Katz case?"

"Ramirez was officially the officer in charge of the Brighton investigation."

"You didn't like his finding?"

"No, and I still don't like it. The more I dug into Katz, the more I realized what a slimeball he had been. Among other unspeakable things, he was a child molester."

"Really! How did you come to that?"

"I came to it by way of Tim Murray. They were old buddies, going back to early childhood. The stories I heard . . . you wouldn't believe it."

"Try me."

"Murray has been screwing his own daughter since she was ten years old."

"Come on!"

"No, I believe it. That comes from the daughter herself. When she was thirteen, her father began sharing her with Harvey Katz."

"What do you mean, sharing . . . ?"

"I mean the three of them romped together. The girl has become very warped, very unstable. She's taking classes at Chaffey this year but what she needs right now is therapy, not education. She—"

"I met her."

"You did?"

"Yeah. Yesterday morning. I was over at Murray's house, went to break the bad news to his widow. Some widow. And some daughter. Those are spectacularly beautiful women, Lila."

"Yes, I think so too. But Patricia has been kept like a bird in a gilded cage. I feel very sorry for her."

"Did she know about the child abuse?"

"I guess not."

"How did you get to it?"

"It just popped out while I was talking to Kelly one day. I was very cautiously probing for information on Katz.

207

Don't even know what it was I said to open her up. Just all of a sudden she was bawling and telling me this horrible story. I had to believe it, Joe."

"How long have you been working with the councilman?"

"How'd you know that?"

"I didn't, until just now. Put it together. He let it drop that he had a 'man' in the department. That was cute. Unless there are more than one working with him. How'd that come about?"

"I approached him. I knew that he had a very low opinion of the chief and was trying to oust him. We had that in common. So I had a talk with him. We've been sharing information, that's all."

"So then you went to Murray."

"Yes. This will sound melodramatic but it was actually very scary. I worked it like a double agent, told Murray that I had been approached by Calhoun, and what should I do?"

"This was when?"

"The day before Murray was fired."

"You had a hand in that?"

"I'd like to think so but, no, I guess not. One of Katz's old pals on the council suddenly switched sides to vote Murray out. That really stunned him. Murray, I mean. He had sort of put me on hold when I first approached him. After he was fired, he called me and told me that he would like to continue our friendship. We met at least once a day every day after that."

"You were doing what for him?"

"Feeding him information, he thought, about Calhoun's plans and strategies, also spreading disinformation, he thought, to the Calhoun camp."

"Where did you usually meet?"

"We usually met at the mansion. That was considered safer than a public place. And of course he was *persona non grata* at the police department, or anywhere around city hall."

"So the story you fed me about . . . how you happened to be invited to the mansion Friday night . . ."

"Yes, I had to lie about that, Joe. I didn't know you from the bogey man."

"But you gave me a great rating with Calhoun."

"I don't know what you're talking about. I have not discussed you with the councilman."

"Sure you haven't?"

"I'm sure I haven't."

"So you'd had your own gate pass for the mansion since when?"

"For about a month."

"Uh huh. Did you disinform me also about your knowledge of Lydia Whiteside?"

"Yes. Actually, I've been cultivating Lydia also. Now there's a number for you. The most truly amoral person I have ever known. Can you handle another cramp in the gut?"

"Let's try it and see."

"She has been getting it on with Kelly Murray. For quite a long time, I gather. Also with Kelly's father, also with Harvey Katz, and every now and then in a romp with all of them together."

"How do you know this, Lila?"

"I heard it first from Kelly."

"First?"

"Uh huh. Then I heard it straight from Lydia herself. She confided to me that she was bisexual, liked it both ways, wondered if I'd ever tried both ways. One thing led to another. I heard enough to confirm Kelly's story."

"Are you bisexual?"

"Me? God, no. And Lydia was after me, boy, let me tell you. That was the hardest part of the whole thing, trying to fend her off without actually shutting her off completely. I learned a lot from Lydia."

"Did you learn a lot from Murray?"

"Not much, no, just enough to keep my curiosity whetted. Yes. He tried to paw me too. I let him, up to a point. Always managed to find a graceful exit at the crucial point. But, boy, that was tough, too."

"What did you learn from Lydia?"

"Well, there is no Harold Schwartzman."

"Uh huh."

"You already knew it?"

"Guessed it."

"The whole thing is a scam. I didn't know that for sure until last night. They started this as—"

"So you were back up there last night. The mansion, I mean."

"Yes, I was up there. I saw Lydia. She met me at the gate. She—"

"At the gate? What time was this?"

"About ten o'clock. She was in a terrible tizzy. I had called her and said that I wanted to come up. She seemed very upset, told me that she would wait for me at the gate."

"This was last night, now, the night that she died."

"Yes. Saturday night. I left Arrowhead shortly behind you. I—"

"Why?"

"Because I felt much better about everything after... after we'd been together. I went up there scared as hell, Joe. People were dying all around me and I still didn't know the good guys from the bad. But I guess you...

reinvigorated me or something. I had to get back into it."

"So you called Lydia and she met you at the gate. Did you go on inside then?"

"No. She had a visitor, in her apartment. I believe it was Kelly Murray. I believe Kelly was freaking out, and Lydia didn't want me to hear what was going on. She needed to talk to me too, though, and that's why she had me come up."

"What did she want to talk to you about?"

"She wanted to know how Tim Murray had died."

"She could have gotten that from the newspaper."

"Yes, but she wanted the real inside story. I gave it to her, as I knew it, and I had to cross my heart and hope to die three times before I could satisfy her. I was there at the gate for maybe five minutes. Then I went looking for you."

"Why?"

"Well, I . . . still wasn't sure about things. Okay, sure about *you*. I wondered if you had killed Murray, Joe."

"Come on, why would I do that?"

"You said you'd come to kick butts."

"Well, sure, but I'm no executioner or vigilante."

"How would I have known what you were? Outside of bed, I mean."

"You'd checked me out. You told Calhoun that I would cut corners but respect the spirit of the law."

"There you go again. I told you I have not discussed you with the councilman."

"You did not go back to the mansion again at eleven o'clock?"

"No."

"You did not go inside, visit Lydia in her apartment?"

"No."

"Then I wonder who did. Another woman came at

211

eleven. Lydia alerted the security guard, told him to pass her through. Who would that be?"

"I haven't the foggiest..."

"What was said during that final talk you had with Lydia that confirmed in your mind that Schwartzman does not exist?"

"Lydia as much as told me so. She said that with Katz and Murray gone, there was no one now but her and she would be the next to die."

"That's where you picked up that phrase."

"Uh huh, it just sort of fell out, I was repeating Lydia's words. I sort of halfway believed it. About myself, I mean. Why not? They were dropping like flies all around me."

"Did you kill a dog Friday night?"

"Yes."

"Why did you change your story?"

"I don't know, except that I became confused and scared. I had already opened the gate and was about to step through when I heard the dog behind me. He was in attack mode, I knew it just from the sound of him. I had my gun in my hand. I whirled and shot him three times. Then I jumped in my car and got the hell away from there."

"Did you tell Murray about that?"

"No. I didn't want him to know I'd been sneaking around up there."

"He knew you had a passkey."

"Of course. He gave it to me a month ago."

"Why do you think Frank Jones was killed?"

"God, I don't know, Joe. I didn't see him that night. But something very important was going on up there Friday night. I believe now that it was a council of war."

"Who do you think was in charge of that?"

"Well, it was not Tim Murray. I went straight from the mansion to Helltown. He was there when I got there."

"How many cops are involved in this?"

"I couldn't give you numbers. But there are a lot involved, to one degree or another. That's a sex club up there, Joe. It may have started as something else, but it's definitely a sex club now. I believe they bring the girls in from Helltown. Lydia was complaining once about the high cost of some of those parties. But I think it might have started as something else."

"Like what?"

"Well . . . for an educated guess . . . a very fancy and very elaborate sting palace, a place to wine and dine and entertain highly placed people in the drug distribution networks."

"Also a place, maybe, to buy and sell?"

"Why not? Or to set up buys somewhere else."

"No, I'm thinking of a safe killing ground. I'm thinking . . ."

"God, Joe!"

"No—try this, Lila. Try it for size. You don't want to make a bust, not a legal one. You merely want to get the buyers in there with heavy bucks, and you want to bury them there, without their bucks. Have you walked those grounds good?"

"God, Joe!"

"We'll need a backhoe, maybe several of them. Start with the flowerbeds. We'll have to . . ."

But I was being premature.

Dale Boyd reminded me of that.

The narcotics team leader stepped into view just outside my one-way window in the back yard. He was dressed for combat and outfitted for annihilation. And he was not alone. I knew all the SWAT hand signals, and I knew that he was positioning his crew for a rush of the house.

So, what the hell.

Nobody lives forever.

But I sure wanted Lila to do so.

CHAPTER 26

I PULLED LILA OUT OF THE SPA and sent her scampering to the bathroom with orders to hit the deck in there and stay there. She took a slight detour past the sofa and scooped up her purse on the run, so at least she was armed though I didn't know what good a little pistol would do her.

I've made it a longstanding practice to keep a loaded and ready riot gun in the bedroom, it's a semi-automatic that delivers a withering pattern of double-ought buck as fast as you can pull the trigger. I snatched it off the wall and took off toward the front of the house dripping naked. It's not the way you'd want to go into combat but there are those times when you have to take it as you find it, and I knew that this was no time to be fooling around with aesthetics.

I figured that I had one small advantage. I knew the combat zone better than the enemy did, and I knew their tactics at least as well as they did. They would stampede through the front door behind an explosive charge that would lay the door on the floor—at least two of them, maybe three—while one or two others tried to find a way in through the rear. Luckily, there were no other ways into this house except to blast through windows or walls, so I felt that I had to meet the charge at the most certain point of entry, then try to handle the rest where the rest would find me.

I took up position in the shadowed hallway with an unobstructed view of the door, checked my weapon, and awaited the inevitable. It was not a long wait. I heard a click and a sizzle at the door, followed instantly by the blast of the explosive charge. Apparently they had not shaped it quite right; it blew the door askew and still hanging in place rather than flat on the floor in front of them, so it was not the cleanest entry possible. Still, they charged straight ahead and there was some momentary confusion in the doorway as they banged around in the cloud of smoke and plaster dust.

I doubt that they ever saw me, and all I saw were shapes in motion. I let go two quick rounds that swept them back out the door. A third round finished the work on the door and it fell out behind them.

Someone yelled out there in a voice of distress. I could hear someone running across the yard—and I thought *oh shit*, wondering how many more there were.

At about that same moment the chatter of an automatic combat rifle erupted at the rear and I heard glass shattering and tinkling.

I skipped back toward the bedroom, saw Lila standing naked in the bathroom doorway with her little snub .38 Detective Special extended and coughing. My whole back wall was gone, a guy in combat fatigues lay twisted and bleeding in the shards of glass, two more were dancing around the yard looking for cover while Lila blasted away at them. "I got one!" she yelled at me.

"Stay covered!" I yelled back, and took off again toward the entryway.

Nothing was happening there so I stepped outside, buck naked, took a quick look at the two who were noisily dying there—recognized both of them, yeah. The one had stood leaning against my office door during the Saturday meeting, with see-everything eyes taking my size. He had a hole in his throat now you could pitch a golfball through and, from the looks of it, those eyes were now trying to see something in a totally different world. The other guy didn't have much chest left; he was a goner too.

I had to step over them both to clear the entrance way, heard feet pounding turf just as I reached the corner of the garage, instinctively dropped to a knee and waited the millisecond it took for the guy to appear. He saw me at, I'm sure, the same time I saw him, with the only difference being in the reflexes and the fact that I was expecting him while he was not expecting me. We fired almost simultaneously but he was off-balance and not quite ready to fire; I was set and waiting, itching to fire.

It was Big Red, Sgt. Dale Boyd, narcotics undercover team leader, and I guess he knew he was a goner even as he was pulling into the trigger of his auto. I saw it all in the eyes, even bluer than I remembered them, and it was the same look he'd given me at the PD as we parleyed only yesterday and he was telling me, "We'd rather it went the other way but ... when it comes, it comes."

The double-ought blast from my riot gun shredded his gun arm and sent him whirling into the ground, his stream of fire punching harmlessly into the heavens as he went. He lay there grunting while his blood soaked into my lawn, within spitting distance from where I knelt. I went over and disarmed him, tossed three weapons into the bushes beside the garage. Our gazes met during that. He smiled, I think, through the red beard and groaned, "Do it one more time, please."

I growled, "Fuck you, guy, do it yourself," and I went on to the rear in support of Lila.

That remarkable gal did not need a lot of support at the moment. She was prancing nakedly about the back lawn, bleeding a bit from a minor cut on the foot—probably picked up as she scrambled through the broken glass to get outside—otherwise doing fine, breathing a bit hard but eyes cool and the emotions under control.

"I got another," she reported. I could see that. The guy was lying on his back in the yard, holding his hands above his face and peering intently at bloodied fingers. "How many are left?"

"Let's check it out," I suggested. "Meet you in front. Go careful. And do *not* fire at a naked man."

We set off in opposite directions to circle the house. I heard her giggle, turned back to see. Our eyes met. She said, "Dammit, Joe, we *are* naked."

"Thanks for noticing," I replied, and we went on about our business, naked notwithstanding.

But it was done.

Lila found another guy lying at the far side, he was full of buck, apparently caught it during the rush on the doorway, no fight left in him now.

We went inside and called the sheriffs. I put a Band-Aid on her foot. We got dressed. The L.A. sheriffs came. The paramedics came. We were in for a long set. After awhile, Captain O'Brien came, then Ralston. With Ralston came Councilman Calhoun, so I knew then who his "man" was. Some time later, the feds came.

We sorted it all out right there.

Then, magically—at about twelve o'clock—every one was gone. Every one, that is, except Lila and me.

I looked at her and said, "Well, that was a short reign."

"What was?" she asked.

"Copp in charge," I explained. "It didn't quite get thirty-six hours."

"That's impossible," she said. "It was longer than that."

I said, "No, from midnight Friday until noon Sunday was all it got."

She said, "Well, God!—Saturday afternoon was three days long! Anyway . . . you're still in charge as far as I'm concerned."

"Really?"

"Uh huh. We'll have to clean up this house. It's in a mess, now. Can you board up the bedroom? And that door—you'll have to fix that door. I'll wash it down but . . ."

I said, "Wait a minute. Which one of us is in charge?"

"You're in charge, Joe," she assured me.

That was another piece of her disinformation, of course. Us guys are never in charge but I guess it can be a nice illusion. I went to board up the bedroom windows and pick up the broken glass. She cleaned up the mess at the entryway and then took a long soak in the spa while I labored on.

But that is what you get when you are the Copp in charge. Of course, you get Lila, too, when the work's all done.

I figured it was a fair push.

BOYD DID NOT die that time but he lost his right arm at the elbow; maybe he would lose the rest after all the murder indictments were handed down. The guy had killed a bunch of people over the past few years, most for profit, and it's guys like these the gas chambers were built for.

Four others in the team survived, two of those wounded in the shootout and two more who'd been driving the getaway vans and took off when the thing went sour. The two wounded men couldn't even wait to get to the hospital to start singing; the D.A. will probably let one or both cop a plea in exchange for their cooperation in the prosecution of Boyd and the others, the others including a couple of sitting city councilmen as well as the other two who'd been in on the thing from the beginning.

As we'd guessed, it may have started clean enough—or almost clean anyway. Katz had seen the amount of riches that were often involved in drug busts in the area, and his displeasure with the way the split usually went between the feds and the cities and counties is a matter of record in the minutes of the council meetings.

It looks like, at first, this was what got them thinking and plotting. Linked to that was a genuine abhorrence and maybe outright hatred vis-à-vis the drug trade in general. Many of the cops shared that frame of mind, had nothing but contempt for the pushers and dealers they encountered routinely in their line of work, resented the soft treatment many were receiving in the courts, were eager and easily enlisted in what may have been perceived by many as a realistic and worthy approach to the problem.

Whatever, it began with the decision to go it alone in the drug wars and a three million dollar appropriation for covert operations. Who knows where the idea came from to build the mansion in the heights? Maybe one of them was a James Bond fan with an appetite for the ridiculous, or maybe all of them thought it would make a splendid statement about the sophistication of a small town turned city almost overnight. Certainly, they threw a lot of money at the police department. It had every technological advantage a department could have, it enjoyed a pay scale far surpassing any other department in the region and a benefits package unparalleled in the state. They had a great facility and what should have been a very happy force—but it was all built upon illusion, and maybe too many of them knew that it was.

I don't know yet exactly what to make of the video tapes Zarraza found in the locked closet of the mansion. It seems sensible to believe that the original intent with the camcorders was geared toward hard evidence during sting operations. They found hidden-camera alcoves behind one-way glass in each of the suites. So maybe it started that way. But it seems that the only evidence on those tapes was the kind that would embarrass the hell out of about fifty of Brighton's best—in compromising sexual activities, to say the least, since most of those guys have wives and a lot have kids. So maybe it was regarded as insurance against faintheartedness on the part of the troops as the intrigue deepened. I don't know, I leave that up to you—what do you think it was? Maybe it was for laughs, or maybe it was for someone's private pleasure. You decide.

For sure, it began to go to hell in a bucket very quickly. Maybe that happened when they stopped policing the drug trade and began merely appropriating it. There is no evidence that the mansion was ever used for a genuine, legal bust. But they're digging up bodies all over the place up there and early readings on the laundry network of offshore bank accounts are pointing toward mega-bucks in ill-gotten gains, perhaps as much as a hundred million.

What do you do with all that money if you're afraid to use it openly? It has been no secret for years now that a lot of narcotics cops in every region of the country have been skimming from the cash found during drug raids. Happens all the time, but they don't get caught until they begin showing conspicuous wealth, and there's the problem. Why take it if you can't spend it? And if you spend it, people will notice and you'll end up in jail. Some of them apparently don't think that far—some cops are real jerks, after all—but that must have been the dilemma of the Brighton coalition, and they must have thought that they had invented the perfect solution.

They invented Harold Schwartzman.

Then, with the help of an executive at the local bank— who turns out to be another old crony—they set up the laundry network. Even then, it was a problem. So they bought properties—some in Baja California, some in Hawaii, some in the Caribbean islands, maybe some others that have not been found yet, certainly quite a few around Brighton—and they actually issued "stock" in Brighton Holding to all the participants. So nobody ever saw a Brighton cop buy a vacation home in Hawaii, but there was always one available. You could visit one of them at their home or search it with a warrant and you'd never find expensive wardrobes, flashy jewelry, or luxury cars— but you'd find those items waiting for whoever got a chance to travel now and then. You'd find Brighton Holding yachts at Newport, Brighton Holding condos and credit accounts at Vegas and other fun capitals—and, at home, you could visit the Schwartzman mansion at regular intervals and party for free with women who were also free.

So why not a happy department, with all that?

Well, you know, you cannot keep something like that going smoothly forever. The more people who are in it, the more chance for dissension and greed and whatever other excess the human expression allows.

And, of course, it was rotten at the top.

Give people like Katz and Murray an inch and they will grab the mile. The illusion of great wealth and power fed their other fantasies, and the fantasies alone could have brought the whole thing down.

Maybe they did.

Couple of items here I need to clear up.

We got this from the cooperating narcs. Franklin Jones was gunned down in cold blood by Dale Boyd because he objected to the clandestine meeting of the "board" which had convened to decide Tim Murray's fate. It happened inside the mansion, probably while Lila was on the grounds. She would not have heard the shots because Boyd had a silencer on the pistol and the report would not have carried beyond the walls.

They had taken him out to bury him beneath the wall when one of the Dobermans "went crazy"—maybe it had the scent of death, and knew whose scent it was—broke out of the kennel and came to investigate. The burial party was no more than thirty feet from the gate when Lila fired at the dog. She fired three shots and fled. Then they saw me coast past in pursuit of Lila. Panic time? Maybe. One of the guys had an inspiration. Jones had been shot three times, too. They buried the dog instead of his keeper and left the body lie, hoping to incriminate Lila in case she had seen what they were doing. Lila unwittingly played into their hands with the story she later concocted as disinformation for my consumption.

The other item has to do with the deaths of Harvey Katz and Tim Murray as well as the death of Lydia Whiteside. Lydia, I think, really did die of an accidental overdose.

I didn't get it straight in my own understanding until the next day, Monday, when Lila and I met Patricia and Kelly Murray at the funeral parlor for a quiet, private wake for their husband and father. The ceremonial police department burial had been canceled as inappropriate in the circumstances. Private burial was scheduled for the following day. The son, Keith, was in a school up north somewhere and apparently had refused to come home for his father's funeral.

Patricia was standing in the vestibule of the small chapel when Lila and I arrived. Kelly was standing alone beside the coffin holding something that looked like a black rose, but I don't know what that was, maybe a silk facsimile. Lila went on down to join the girl and I stayed to talk to Patricia.

"How is she taking it?" I asked the mother.

"Not bad," she replied in a soft voice. "Considering . . ."

Even in black she looked spectacular.

I told her, "We'll have to take Kelly with us when we leave."

"Do you have to do that?"

"Yes. Not to serve the ends of justice, necessarily. I believe that has already been done. But for her own sake. She will need help, Patricia."

"Yes, I suppose she will."

"When did you learn about the abuse?"

"For sure? Saturday night."

"When you went up to see Lydia?"

"Yes. She called me at home. Told me I needed to come pick up my daughter."

"Did she tell you why?"

"She told me that Kelly was strung out and acting crazy.

She couldn't do anything with her. So I went up there and took Kelly home."

"What had been going on up there that night, Patricia?"

"I don't know. Kelly was totally naked, full of drugs, wandering around with blank eyes, walking into walls, couldn't be still. I couldn't even get her dressed. Finally I just wrapped her in a blanket and Lydia helped me get her into the car."

"What sort of shape was Lydia in?"

"Not much better than Kelly, I guess. She was staggering around and talking a little crazy herself. Popping pills all the time I was there. Why do people do that to themselves? Is that supposed to be fun or entertaining?"

"How long were you up there?"

"I don't know. Fifteen, twenty minutes maybe. Seemed like hours, though. Lydia had told me to come around to the back of the house to her private entrance. I did. She let me in. Kelly didn't even know I was there. Lydia kept telling me that she'd gone crazy. She pulled me over to this portable typewriter in the bedroom and told me to look at the note Kelly had written. I thought Kelly could not have written that. She couldn't even see."

"Maybe earlier, though."

"Yes, probably earlier. I gather she'd been there all evening."

"Did you see the gun?"

"Yes. It was next to the typewriter."

"Recognize it?"

"Yes. It has a cracked handle. One of Tim's old guns."

"So you knew."

"Well, no, but I was ready to be convinced. Kelly took care of that yesterday. She said that it was true."

"She killed her father."

"Yes. And Harvey Katz."

"Did she tell you why?"

"She told me about the abuse. She was never forced, Joe. I believe that is why it is so . . . destructive for her now. She hated it, oh she hated it, and as she grew older she hated herself for it. But still there was . . . well, it had a . . . a strange appeal."

"Did she tell you how she killed Harvey?"

"Yes. He had sent for her. She was to meet him in that motel. When she got there, this other girl was there with Harvey, a prostitute. She knew the girl would be there. He'd told her when he called Kelly to join them. She took her father's gun. And she killed them."

"Did she say why?"

"Not in any coherent way. But I think she was just trying to kill that part of her life."

"Did Tim know?"

"Yes. She told him about it. He covered it up. From what she told me yesterday, I gathered that he destroyed some evidence at the scene that would have implicated Kelly. I don't know . . . maybe that gave her some peace. For a little while. I didn't know why at the time but she was very different after that. She'd been having emotional problems. But they cleared up like a snap of the fingers and she started college on opening day. Everything seemed beautiful."

"For about a month."

"Yes, for about a month. Then she started with the dreams again."

"What kind of dreams?"

"Horrible dreams, I guess."

"Tim was at her again."

Patricia sighed heavily. "Yes, it seems that he was. Kelly

lives near the campus. Tim went there the other night after he got off work. He—"

"Friday night?"

"Yes—well, Saturday morning. He got her out of bed and they went driving around. She must have known what he wanted because she took the gun with her. She shot him in the park, put his body in the trunk of the car, then drove it back and parked it outside his work. She called me from a pay phone and I picked her up."

"Did she tell you what happened?"

"Yes. But she told it as a dream."

"Dreams don't take you to Helltown."

"Hers could. Often she walks in her dreams, even drives cars in her dreams."

"But she is not really dreaming?"

"Well, I think she has trouble discerning one state from another."

Lila had an arm around the girl and they were heading our way. I said, "Thank you, Patricia."

"Be gentle with her."

"You know we will."

"Yes. Joe . . . I took Tim's money to the PD this morning."

"It's best that way. Has blood all over it."

"Yes. I could hardly touch it, let alone spend it. And, uh, please forgive the vulgar way I spoke to you the other day. I just did not know how to otherwise express such vulgarity."

"I understand," I told her. "Be that direct with Keith."

"What?"

"You'll need to talk to him, Patricia. God knows what he may be hiding from, within himself. Talk to him. Soon."

227

"Thank you. And thank you for understanding."

"I do," I said, and I did.

We took Kelly Murray to the PD and Lila booked her, then we took her to the hospital and checked her in. She was like a child—a ten-year-old child—and I doubt that she even knew what was going on, except perhaps as a dream.

It's not a pretty story, is it? Few are, in my line of work. But it's my world, and I try to stay in charge of it whenever I can.

Speaking of ugly, my little allegory about the pirates and the mutiny was closer than I realized at the time. Boyd had been responsible for the firing of Tim Murray, it was part of the insurrection that had already started before I came on the scene. This councilman, Lofton, switched his vote after a visit from Boyd. I don't know what was said to change his mind, but Murray was fired that same night. Of course, Lofton and the others of the "old guard" are facing charges in several venues, including federal, so each will reap what has been sown, be assured of that.

I'm in Arrowhead at the moment. Lila's here, too, and we've been doing a lot of walking along the lakeshore, eating piles of steak sandwiches at Woody's Boathouse, and getting to know each other in all the subtle ways. Jack Ralston has been appointed Acting Chief at Brighton and old pal Carl Garcia came out of hiding to reclaim his job. Calhoun seems a cinch to win the upcoming special election for mayor and it looks like his whole slate will be running things before long. I believe Brighton will survive its coming of age and go on to be one of the model cities of the region.

Many new faces at the PD already, of course. Zarraza was made a sergeant of detectives and he's actually running the homicide detail until everything shakes out in the reorganization. Ramirez is gone, a lot of them are gone, and a lot of them will be facing charges in the days ahead. Some are already behind bars—a couple of patrol teams and a dispatcher, in particular, in connection with the ambush of Hanson and Rodriguez, which of course was ordered by Boyd as the new "chairman of the board."

I can drop in there any time I like, now, and get a nice reception. Many of those guys were damned glad to see the shakeup come down, and some of them still call me Chief. Funny, isn't it? Never saw myself as a Chief, forever an Indian. Naw, I'd make a terrible chief. I get bored too easy, and I can't stand the politics.

Sort of enjoy having a partner, though, after all this time. Maybe I fall in love too easy, too, but what is a world without love? I believe Lila is looking over my shoulder as I write this. She wants to go to the Boathouse and rape another Woody's steak sandwich.

I could do that.

What the hell. I'd love to do that.